LOST INNOCENCE

DI SALLY PARKER #5

M A COMLEY

JEAMLE PUBLISHING LIMITED

OTHER BOOKS BY M A COMLEY

Blind Justice (Novella)

Cruel Justice (Book #1)

Mortal Justice (Novella)

Impeding Justice (Book #2)

Final Justice (Book #3)

Foul Justice (Book #4)

Guaranteed Justice (Book #5)

Ultimate Justice (Book #6)

Virtual Justice (Book #7)

Hostile Justice (Book #8)

Tortured Justice (Book #9)

Rough Justice (Book #10)

Dubious Justice (Book #11)

Calculated Justice (Book #12)

Twisted Justice (Book #13)

Justice at Christmas (Short Story)

Prime Justice (Book #14)

Heroic Justice (Book #15)

Shameful Justice (Book #16)

Immoral Justice (Book #17)

Unfair Justice (a 10,000 word short story)

Irrational Justice (a 10,000 word short story)

Seeking Justice (a 15,000 word novella)

Clever Deception (co-written by Linda S Prather)

Tragic Deception (co-written by Linda S Prather)

Sinful Deception (co-written by Linda S Prather)

Forever Watching You (DI Miranda Carr thriller)

Wrong Place (DI Sally Parker thriller #1)

No Hiding Place (DI Sally Parker thriller #2)

Cold Case (DI Sally Parker thriller#3)

Deadly Encounter (DI Sally Parker thriller #4)

Lost Innocence (DI Sally Parker thriller #5)

Web of Deceit (DI Sally Parker Novella with Tara Lyons)

The Missing Children (DI Kayli Bright #1)

Killer On The Run (DI Kayli Bright #2)

Hidden Agenda (DI Kayli Bright #3)

Murderous Betrayal (Kayli Bright #4)

Dying Breath (Kayli Bright #5)

The Caller (co-written with Tara Lyons)

Evil In Disguise – a novel based on True events

Deadly Act (Hero series novella)

Torn Apart (Hero series #1)

End Result (Hero series #2)

In Plain Sight (Hero Series #3)

Double Jeopardy (Hero Series #4)

Sole Intention (Intention series #1)

Grave Intention (Intention series #2)

Devious Intention (Intention #3)

Merry Widow (A Lorne Simpkins short story)

It's A Dog's Life (A Lorne Simpkins short story)

A Time To Heal (A Sweet Romance)

A Time For Change (A Sweet Romance)

High Spirits

The Temptation series (Romantic Suspense/New Adult Novellas)

Past Temptation

Lost Temptation

KEEP IN TOUCH WITH THE AUTHOR:

Twitter
https://twitter.com/Melcom1

Blog
http://melcomley.blogspot.com

Facebook
http://smarturl.it/sps7jh

Newsletter
http://smarturl.it/8jtcvv

BookBub
www.bookbub.com/authors/m-a-comley

ACKNOWLEDGMENTS

Thank you as always to my rock, Jean, I'd be lost
without you in my life.

Special thanks as always go to my talented editor Stefanie Spangler
Buswell and to Studioenp their superb cover design expertise.

My heartfelt thanks go to my wonderful proofreaders Joseph Calleja
and Emmy Ellis @ Studioenp for spotting all the lingering nits.

And finally, to all the wonderful Bloggers and Facebook groups
for their never-ending support of my work.

Thank you to Steven Jay for allowing me to use his name in this book.

PROLOGUE

JEFF RYLAND and the group of boys he hung out with dispersed, all keen to get home for their tea after the adventure they had just been on. After leaving school and dumping his schoolbag, he'd joined up with them, like usual, for a couple of hours. His parents, just like most parents, were eager to get the boys out from under their feet, so any homework they had would be completed in between having their evening meal and bedtime.

The small woodland close to the estate where he lived was an absolute treasure, full of secret nooks. Some of them, the boys had only recently discovered, adding to the group's excitement.

Jeff hung around with five other lads his age. Most of the time, they behaved and avoided getting into trouble by keeping themselves adequately occupied. They were often classed as a mischievous crowd rather than a troublesome one.

On a Thursday in May nineteen eighty-five, after saying farewell to the rest of the group, Jeff was busy kicking at stones and generally dawdling on his way back home. His mum would be late—she always was on Thursdays because she cared for her ill father in the afternoon, giving the regular carer some much-needed time off. His father worked long shifts at a factory and wasn't around much during the week, while his older brothers did their own thing after school, which always excluded him.

Up ahead, an older group of kids hung out on the street corner. Jeff's pace stalled, and he considered crossing the road to avoid walking past them, but his mother's warning about crossing High Common Road when it was busy prevented him. He swallowed hard, placed his hands in his pockets, dropped his head and marched ahead.

He could feel the group staring at him. He'd caught a few words they were saying before they fell silent as he got closer. It sounded as though they intended to rob one of the local shops.

Shit! I need to keep my head down and ignore them.

A smaller lad with ginger hair put paid to that plan when he intentionally stood in Jeff's path.

Jeff mumbled an apology when he bumped into him.

The boy shoved him hard in the chest. "Oi! What do you think you're doing? Didn't you see me?"

Jeff gulped loudly. His chin on his chest, he said, "I'm sorry. I wasn't looking where I was going. I'm going to be late for my tea. Sorry." He tried to manoeuvre around the boy, but the lad obstructed him.

The rest of the gang roared with laughter—all except one boy who Jeff knew really well. He glanced sideways and issued a silent plea to the other boy, who turned away and refused to come to Jeff's assistance.

The ginger-haired lad prodded Jeff's chest—harsh jabs that intensified with each touch. "I want to hear you apologise, squirt."

Jeff sighed and let out a juddering breath. His words caught in his throat and he apologised under his breath again.

The ginger lad punched Jeff's upper arm and leaned in close. "I can't hear you, dipshit."

Jeff closed his eyes, forcing the tears back. He feared his heart was about to jump out of his chest. The beat had become erratic, and breathing was difficult. He was prone to having panic attacks, so he knew that if he didn't slow his breathing down, an attack would be imminent. With the lout goading him and the rest of the gang egging him on, Jeff didn't see how he could. Again, he glanced sideways at the boy he knew. The other boy's head dropped, and he shuffled his feet, obviously feeling embarrassed by the situation.

"I said I'm sorry. Please let me pass. I need to get home."

"Aww…did you hear what the petrified mouse said? He needs to get home. Probably wants to cry in his mummy's apron. Is that right, pipsqueak?"

"No. My mother isn't at home…" His voice trailed off when he realised what he'd just said.

Numbskull, why don't I learn to keep my mouth shut?

"Is that right? Well, maybe you want to hang out with us for a little while, eh? That'd be fun, right?"

"I can't. I'm sorry, not tonight. I'd love to another day. Just not tonight." He raised his head a little, enough to see the ginger boy's anger flare up in his ruddy cheeks.

"Refusing to hang out with us—do you really think that's an option, squirt?"

Jeff's breathing notched up a little. His small chest expanded and deflated rhythmically. "Please, I have to go. I don't want to be late."

"Late for what? You've already told us that your mummy isn't at home. Who else is there waiting for you?" The ginger lad's question was accompanied by a flat-handed jab to Jeff's midriff.

He doubled over in pain, tears pricking his eyes. He was at a loss for what to do next. If he ran, they would give chase and catch up with him before he got a few feet, so that wasn't an option. Running out of ideas, he again glanced sideways at the boy he knew. He avoided eye contact altogether, though. Jeff's heart sank from his chest.

Help me, please!

The other boys laughed, mocking Jeff and calling him vile names.

"Let's use him," the gang leader said.

Jeff knew the leader only by his nickname, which was Fletch, after Fletcher from the TV show *Porridge*. Jeff swivelled his head to look at Fletch. He turned away quickly at the boy's scowl. It was too late—Jeff's actions had obviously angered Fletch.

A moment later, Fletch was standing beside Jeff, only inches away.

He had little control over his body and felt the panic rising up from the pit of his stomach, constricting his heart, and venturing into his throat. He tried to speak, but the words failed to form. He was in danger of passing out and his breath failed to find its normal course through his nose.

"You up for a little job, squirt?"

Fletch's hot breath brushed the side of his face, and Jeff closed his eyes. He was petrified, getting more and more scared with each passing second. "Please, I just want to go home. I have homework. I need to do it before I go to school tomorrow."

The gang laughed. All except one. Jeff glanced his way again, silently sending out a plea for help.

The boy did nothing. He just stood there, watching those around him as if he was too afraid to admit to the gang that he knew Jeff.

Not wanting the situation to become worse than it already was, Jeff decided not to dob the boy in. He had a feeling the boy would come to his rescue if Jeff really needed his help.

Or is that just wishful thinking?

Fletch took another step forward and placed an arm around Jeff's shoulders, squeezing him so hard that any breath he had in his tiny body was immediately forced out. He tried to replace the breath, but his fear got in the way. With no oxygen left in his lungs, his focus blurred. Confused, he had no idea how to breathe for himself any longer. Fletch's grip tightened even more. The panic overwhelmed him before Fletch could give him instructions what to do next. Jeff's legs gave way. The group laughed again when he ended up on the ground at Fletch's size-eight feet.

Finally, the boy he knew stepped forward and tried to help. "Leave the lad alone, Fletch. We're wasting time on him. We've got a job to do, remember?"

"You're right." Fletcher turned to the ginger lad and said, "Ging, get rid of him. Take him in the alley and knock seven bells of shit out of him and send him on his way."

The ginger lad grabbed Jeff by the scruff, forcing him to his feet.

"Please, I don't want any trouble. Let me go. I promise I won't tell anyone," Jeff pleaded.

Fletcher reached out and placed a hand around Jeff's throat, cutting off his breath. Jeff clawed at Fletch's hands, trying to pry his fingers loose. "You better not, boy. Take your punishment like a man. Now go, get out of my sight." He cast Jeff aside forcefully.

Jeff staggered as Ginger pushed him. His shoe fell off, and he scrabbled to pick it up before Ginger grasped his arm and continued to shove him along the road and into the alley a few feet away.

"The boy done bad talking to Fletch like that. No one—you hear me?—*no one* talks back to Fletch. That's disrespectful, squirt. And disrespect warrants a slap. Now be a good boy and take what's coming to you, and I'll let you go in a second or two. If you fight me or try to run away, you'll only make things worse for yourself, got that?"

Jeff sniffled, tears streaming down his face at the thought of what lay ahead of him.

The blows came thick and fast. It wasn't long before his body refused to take any more. His legs buckled, and he dropped to the ground. Once Jeff was down, Ginger used his foot. Not gentle taps but large, heavy swings of the legs, aimed at Jeff's stomach, chest and head. Jeff's breathless pleas went unheard. It wasn't long before everything became dazed. He could feel himself slipping into unconsciousness.

Before everything went totally black, a familiar voice shouted, "Jesus, what have you done, you fucking moron? What have you done? Jeff? Jeff, are you all right?"

CHAPTER 1

SALLY PARKER WAS in the process of tearing apart the lounge. "Where did I put my damn handbag? Simon, have you seen it?"

She glanced up. Her grinning fiancé was leaning against the door-frame, her handbag thrown over his shoulder. He entered the room, swaying his hips as he walked towards her. "Does it suit me? I've often thought about investing in one of those man bags."

Sally laughed then straightened her face. "You buy one of them, Mr. Pathologist, and you can kiss our wedding goodbye."

His face was a picture, and his mouth gaped open for a few seconds before Sally laughed.

"You really can be the most gullible man at times."

He threw her bag on the couch and reached for her, pulling her into his arms. "Gullible, am I? Hey, if I didn't know you any better, I'd think you keep making up all these excuses intentionally so as not to marry me. A man could easily get a complex, you know."

"What? Does that mean I'm not even allowed to make a joke any more?"

"Jokes are okay, but there's also that saying 'many a true word is spoken in jest'. It does make me wonder sometimes if you truly want to be Mrs. Sally Bracknall. After all, it's been a year since I asked you to be my wife."

Sally leaned back, her gaze meeting his. "Are you serious? Simon, you know how much I love you. Dad's accident put paid to our initial wedding plans. You know that. We both agreed it would be better to postpone the wedding until he was better."

"He was better a few months later."

Sally had trouble figuring out if Simon was being serious or not. "But then your business took off, and the extra hours you and Dad were putting in on the houses got in the way. That's what delayed things—not me."

He kissed her tenderly. "I know. I was only messing with you. Right. Tonight, we make a deal and sit down properly to discuss the wedding, okay?"

Sally extracted herself from his arms and opened the coffee table drawer. She withdrew a huge file and placed it on the surface. "The wedding folder. I'll leave it here to act as a reminder for when we come home this evening."

"I'm thinking we should forget all about that and just elope. I hear they do a decent service up in Gretna Green, if you're willing to give it a go."

"What? Are you serious? Or are you winding me up again?" she asked, because Simon *did* have a penchant for doing just that at times.

"Although I was joking," he said, "maybe we should consider it, with money being so tight at present. Of course, our immediate families need to be there. They'd probably lynch us if we truly eloped and didn't invite them."

"Reading between the lines—what you're really trying to tell me is that you're too tight to fork out for a wedding with all the bells and whistles."

"I am *not*. If it came to the crunch, I would apply for a loan if I had to."

"What a great way to start off married life—with a huge loan over our heads. And there was me thinking you were rolling in the green stuff."

His mouth gaped open again.

Sally sniggered. "Catching flies won't help. Surely you don't think I was being serious."

He shook his head and smiled. "Not in the slightest," he said unconvincingly.

"I've got to dash, and you should be going, too. We'll sit down and thrash this out when we get home this evening, all right?" She kissed him, picked up her handbag and rushed out the front door.

He appeared on the doorstep when she approached her car. "See you later, Sally. I love you, no matter what we decide."

"Ditto, Simon. I'd be lost without you around to wind up every day. Have a good one." She gave him a toothy grin.

He smiled and shook his head. "You, too."

Sally set off for Wymondham Police Station, which was a good twenty-minute drive from Simon's plush home. She caught herself smiling when she reflected on how lucky she was to have him in her life after her divorce. She cringed as Darryl's sneering face entered her mind. She was well shot of him, thank goodness. He was locked away in the depths of a prison in the Highlands in Scotland, for not only sexually assaulting her but also for interfering with another prisoner she was trying to help.

That prisoner's case was the first of many Sally had been tasked with investigating after a retired police officer's gross misconduct had come to light. Her team, which had been part of the murder squad, had become a cold case team. Once their investigations began in earnest, it soon became apparent that dozens of innocent people were languishing in prison because of DI Falkirk and his appalling actions.

Over the past year, Sally's team had solved ten of the cold cases, but a hundred or so were still awaiting reinvestigation. Their efforts had managed to secure the release of eight prisoners—all men who had been wrongly convicted due to Falkirk's lack of investigative prowess. Though she was delighted to give the men their freedom back, it sickened her to think how many years behind bars those innocent people had been forced to endure. DI Falkirk had a lot to answer for. She was elated when she heard that the force had stripped him of his pension. In Sally's eyes, *he* should be the one sitting behind bars. However, her superiors hadn't seen it that way. They felt stripping the former inspector of his pension was punishment enough for his carelessness and lack of professionalism.

Sally drew into the station and found her partner, Jack Blackman, resting against the bonnet of his car. His arms folded, he was waiting for her.

"Hi, Jack. Lovely morning. How's things?"

He pulled a face and scratched the stubble he was trying to grow into a beard. "Fair to middling. How about you?"

"Good, thanks. I'm dying for a cup of coffee. We can have a chat over that if you need to."

"I'm fine. Nothing you can say or do will ever change my situation."

"Ouch, at least let me try. Are things really that bad at home?"

He shrugged and launched himself off the bonnet of his car. "Oh, I don't know. It's probably me blowing things up out of all proportion. Why on earth did Donna and I decide to have kids?"

"I'm sure, deep down, you don't really mean that, mate. Every parent must feel like that at one time or another."

"You're probably right. Hey, if you take my advice, you'll steer clear of having them when you and that pathologist fiancé of yours finally tie the knot. Any news on that, by the way? I could do with a good knees-up."

They took a few steps towards the entrance of the station before she answered, "As a matter of fact, we're going to sit down and discuss the plans tonight. I have the wedding folder primed and ready for action."

"Ha, all that expense. I know if I had my chance to do things again, I would have tried my hardest to persuade Donna to elope. Gretna's not that far away—a few hours, that's all."

Sally giggled.

"Something I said?" he asked.

"I was just wondering how many times that conversation came up between men over a pint down the pub."

He frowned. "Sorry, what's that supposed to mean?"

"It's just that Simon and I had the very same conversation before I left the house this morning."

He stopped mid-flight up the stairs. "What? He wants to elope?"

"Keep your voice down, Jack. Like I said, nothing is set in stone, and we're going to sit down tonight to discuss things further. I'm not sure how I feel about the proposal yet." They continued up the stairs. "I get the money aspect of things and what else we could do with the funds, but I'd miss not having my friends at the wedding."

"Yeah, try and dissuade him. I need a good excuse to get pissed."

Sally tutted and shook her head. "You men and your bloody beer."

"Beer? I was thinking more along the lines of the hard stuff. Hey, here's a thought—you could hire a coach and ship us all up to Gretna for the weekend. We could all be at the wedding, then we could take in one of those distillery tours afterwards. I enjoy a nice drop of malt."

Sally pushed open the incident room door and stepped through it. "Ain't gonna happen, Bullet." She used the nickname he'd inherited from his army days. He'd been Sally's partner for around nine years, and he always claimed being a copper was safer than being a soldier, as he'd been shot four times during his stint in the army.

"Shame. Don't ever say I don't come up with good ideas, though. I thought it was ace. I'm sure the guys around here would agree with me, too, if you ran the idea past them."

Sally chose to ignore his final comment and headed towards DC Joanna Tryst's desk. Joanna was obviously distracted by something on her computer, as she didn't turn to say good morning like she usually did. Sally was keen to know what was drawing her interest. "Morning, Joanna. Anything wrong?"

Joanna fell back in her chair and placed a hand over her chest. "Damn, I didn't hear you come in. Sorry, boss."

"Sorry to scare you. Is everything all right?" Sally leaned over her shoulder to peer at the screen.

"Just doing my usual morning trawl through the wires, boss. There was a murder overnight that caught my interest."

A familiar twinge knotted deep in Sally's gut. "Hey, the quicker we go through all these cold cases, the sooner we can get back to real policing. Ugh...I can't believe those words tumbled out of my mouth. You know what I mean. It's often harder for us piecing all the clues together on cold cases. I sometimes have to remind myself that the necessity is there for us to put all the wrongs right. Especially when I hear of a meaty investigation rearing its head."

"I enjoy the cold cases, boss, but like you say, people don't realise how difficult our job is at times, and the work can be extremely frustrating and mind-numbing in equal quantities."

Sally smiled, placed a hand on Joanna's shoulder and squeezed. "I totally get where you're coming from. I have days when a case seems futile. However, when we get a breakthrough that helps us crack the case, the old familiar buzz takes over. We've all done well in the past year, solving the cases we have. Just think of all those people we've set free from prison in that time. I do, and sometimes, that's what gives me the impetus to carry on with these cold cases. Hey, look on the bright side—not that you were being negative at all—the rate we're going, we should have all these cases completed in the next five years."

Jack groaned behind her. "Did you have to say that?"

Sally wished she could have bitten her tongue in half for telling the truth. When they'd started up the cold case team, Jack had been the one person opposed to the idea and had even threatened to leave her team at one point. But Sally and DCI Mike Green had persuaded Jack to stay on. Most of the time, Sally remained upbeat about the investigations they were working for fear of any backlashes coming from her partner. He still managed to have a little moan now and again if a case was proving too frustrating, though. "It's a fact, Jack. Unless we start putting in extra hours to solve the cases."

"It's not that easy, boss. You know that."

Sally nodded. "I know. We need to work with the hand we've been dealt and get on with things to the best of our ability. I want more genuinely innocent people like Craig Gillan out from behind bars as quickly as humanly possible. You must admit, big man, you got a buzz from setting him free as much as I did."

Jack shrugged. "I suppose so. The guy was dealt a raw deal by his brother in more ways than one. Glad he's free and enjoying life once again with his family."

"There you go. See how easy it is to turn a negative into a positive? None of us like going over old ground, but we see the need for us to do it. Especially if the ground wasn't picked over properly in the first place." Sally sighed.

They'd all had similar conversations over the past year. It was time they got past the negatives and got on with the task in hand: freeing innocent people who had been wrongly convicted. Her eyes brimmed with tears every time she thought of the first man they'd freed. The last she'd heard, Craig and his two children were seriously getting to know each other by going on several holidays thanks to the large sum of compensation they'd received due to his false imprisonment. They had also bought a large house together with ten acres of land. Because Craig had always fancied himself as a bit of a farmer, he'd filled his acreage with different animals, everything from chickens to alpacas. The family were all thrilled with their new life and the challenges animal husbandry brought to them daily. Sally was elated for them.

That case was a prime example of why the cold cases sitting in Sally's office were so important. Otherwise, innocent people doing time behind bars for a crime they didn't commit would prey on her conscience for years.

"I'll be in my office for the next ten minutes. I have a few notes I need to type up on the last case we solved, then we'll figure out what we should do next. Jack, do you want to grab a handful of files from my office? Select a couple of worthy ones we can sink our teeth into?"

"Will do." Jack entered her office.

Sally stopped off at the vending machine and chose a white coffee. She walked into her office to find Jack crouching on the floor next to the pile of files that were gathering dust below her window.

"I think we've pretty much tackled the larger cases, if I recall. I'll sift through this lot with Joanna and see which ones we should choose next."

"Good. I won't be long."

Jack spent the next few minutes searching through the files then left the office with a handful of them.

As she scribbled down her notes, Sally's mind wandered back to her wedding. Maybe Jack had the right idea after all. Perhaps it would be great to hire a coach and bus everyone up to Scotland for a few days. It would be a darn sight cheaper in the long run.

She wasn't long into her note-taking when an excited Joanna appeared in the doorway. "Sorry to interrupt, boss. I have a Harry Rogers on the line for you."

Sally recognised the name but was unsure where from. "Do I know him?"

"Sorry, I should have added his rank. It's DS Harry Rogers. He would like a quick chat about a case he's just taken on."

"Great, as if I haven't got enough to do, other officers contact me, expecting me to do their work for them, as well."

Joanna's mouth twisted. "I don't think it's quite like that, boss. I think you should hear what he has to say."

"That's very cryptic. Why all the secrecy, Joanna?"

Joanna smiled and backed out of the door. "I'll put the call through to you."

Sally tapped her pen on the desk until her phone rang. "DI Sally Parker. How can I help, DS Rogers?"

"Hello, ma'am. I'm at a crime scene and was told by the desk sergeant to get in touch with you."

"You were? May I ask why? Or are you expecting me to guess?" Sally asked, her impatience obvious in her tone.

"It looks like a cold case, ma'am. Forgive me if I'm wrong, but that's your department, isn't it?"

"You're right. I do run a cold case team, but we have several cases vying for our attention as it is without adding more to our load."

"Okay. I'll deal with the case myself then, if you're not interested."

Sally sighed. "Wait a minute. Okay, you've grabbed my attention. I never said I wasn't interested."

"That's great. Any chance you can pop down here then, ma'am?"

Sally exhaled a large breath and sought out a clean sheet of paper. With her pen poised, she said, "Go on then, give me the details."

Rogers reeled off the address. "Will you be joining me soon, ma'am?"

"Yes, and when I get there, you can cut the 'ma'am' crap. It makes me feel old and decrepit, and I'm far from that."

"Rightio, DI Parker."

"That's better. My partner and I will see you soon. Have you rung the pathologist?"

"Yes, he's en route. ETA around ten minutes."

"We should be there in twenty-five to thirty minutes, unless we get held up by a tractor at this time of year."

"Nothing bad on the road when I was called out. I'll see you soon, ma'am…sorry, habit."

"One I hope you manage to break before I see you later. Thanks for ringing, DS Rogers." Sally hung up and left her chair. Walking back into the incident room, she said, "Jack, leave those. We're wanted elsewhere. I'll fill you in on the way. Joanna, would you mind sifting through the files instead, in case we need one or two cases later?"

"On it, boss."

"Jordan and Stuart, while we're out, can you finish up the case we were dealing with last week? Ensure all the evidence is listed and all the i's have been dotted, et cetera. It would be nice to have a clear desk for a change before another case comes our way."

Both men nodded.

"Ready, Jack?" Sally asked, pushing through the door.

"I'm coming. See you later, guys," he called out to the rest of the team.

CHAPTER 2

WHEN SHE AND Jack arrived at the small estate in the village of Swanton Morley, Sally was immediately struck by the lack of houses in the quiet location. The house where Rogers had asked to meet them was a mid-terrace that dated back to the early 1900s, according to the date stone above the door. A young uniformed officer asked to see their IDs before he allowed them access to the building. Once inside, Sally and Jack walked through the hallway and the kitchen and out the back door into the medium-sized garden.

Simon greeted Sally and Jack the instant he saw them. "I'm glad you two were called in on this case."

Standing alongside him was a heavy-set man wearing a black suit who appeared to be in his fifties.

"You must be DS Rogers?" Sally asked.

"I am. Thanks so much for coming, DI Parker. I'm sure this case will be of interest to you."

"Can you tell me what we're seeing here?" Sally asked, scanning the area, her gaze drawn to a mound of earth and a pile of wood that looked like a dilapidated shed off to one side of the garden.

"The new owners of the house decided to pull down their shed and erect a new one but found the concrete base in a bad state of repair.

They dug up the base then left it overnight. In the morning, they returned to find that animals had disturbed the earth and dug up some bones. The woman is a nurse at the hospital and instantly identified the bones as human. Her husband rang the station immediately. The case landed on my desk when I got into work this morning around eight. I drove out here right away and got the ball rolling by ringing you and the pathologist. That's as far as I got."

Sally ran a finger and thumb around her chin. "Simon? Anything to add, or is it too early?"

"The only thing I can tell you for definite at present is that I can concur—the bones are human. My team are going to take a while excavating the site. I won't be able to give you any hint of what age or sex the victim is until we piece all the bones together back at the lab."

Exhaling a large breath, Sally took a step closer to the mound. "Any inkling as to when the body was buried?"

"Not at this point, Sally," Simon replied from behind her.

"There must be something for us to go on?"

"Okay, if you want me to stretch my neck out and take a punt, I would say we're dealing with the remains of either a pre-teen or a small woman. That's as much as I'm willing to divulge at this point. Don't blame me if that information changes farther down the line after I've assembled all the bones together. Which, pre-empting your next question, could take weeks rather than days."

Sally grinned at Simon. He really did know her too well. "But you'll do your best to rush the results through, won't you?" She gave him her most dazzling smile.

He shook his head and laughed. "I'll do my best. You know that."

"I know. We'll leave you to it then and have a word with the owner of the house. That is if you don't mind, DS Rogers?"

"Why should I mind? Aren't you taking over the case from now on?"

"Let's not get ahead of ourselves here. This might be a recent murder, one that our team can't get involved in. We won't know that until the pathologist issues his report."

Simon cleared his throat. "Sorry, I should have said I believe the body could have been in situ for the past twenty years or more."

Sally's eyes widened. "Wow, well, that certainly changes the structure of the case. Okay, Rogers, you've got your wish if you want to hand over the reins."

The policeman seemed relieved. "Excellent news. I'll leave the case in your safe hands then, ma'am."

Sally rolled her eyes. "Go on, off with you. Before you go, I need the name of the proprietors."

"Mrs. Sara Walden. You'll find her next door at number five."

"Thanks, Sergeant."

Sally and Jack retraced their steps through the house and knocked on the front door of the neighbour's property.

An elderly woman with a walking frame opened the door. "Hello, are you the police?" she asked, her voice quaking.

"Yes, is it possible to have a word with Mrs. Walden please?"

"You best come in. I'll lead the way if you'll shut the door behind you."

When the woman turned and started the slow journey up the dated hallway, Sally smiled at Jack before setting off after her at a snail's pace.

They eventually reached the lounge and found a woman in her thirties on the sofa, sniffling. She glanced up as they entered the room.

"Sara, there are two police officers to see you, dear. Do you want me to stay?"

"If you would, Vera, thank you."

"Hello, Sara. Please, I want to reassure you there's nothing for you to worry about. I'd also like to thank you for contacting us. Are you up to answering some questions? I know what a shock this must be for you. We'll be out of your hair in no time at all, I promise you."

"You might be, but what about the forensic team? Will they want to tear my house apart, too? We've only been here a couple of months. We've worked tirelessly to get the inside finally straight, and now this."

"They'll need to conduct a thorough search of your property. I'm sorry about that, but I'm sure you can understand how important their work is in a case like this."

"I do. It doesn't make me feel any better, though. I knew we shouldn't have moved here. I said to Brian there was something about the house that didn't sit well with me. He insisted I was being silly and forced me to go ahead with the purchase." She ran a shaking hand over her colourless cheek.

"It's funny how some people can pick up on a house's energy better than others. Hopefully, the inside of the house will prove to be free of any further remains, then you'll be able to get on with your lives soon."

"No way. I'm moving out as soon as I'm able to get my personal belongings. There's no way I could live there now. Sorry, Vera, I hate to say that after you being so kind to us the last few months."

Vera patted Sara's hand. "Nonsense, lovey. I understand. I'm sure I would feel the same way you do if I were in your shoes."

Sally nodded. "I completely understand, too. Maybe you can give me the name of your solicitor. I'll need to trace the deeds for the property to see who the previous owners have been over the years. According to the pathologist, the bones might have been down there as long as twenty years or more."

Vera gasped. "Never! Oh my. How dreadful, to think I've lived here all that time with a body lying mere feet away from me."

"You have? That's interesting, Vera. I don't suppose you could help us with the names of the people who have owned the house over the years?"

The older woman chewed on her lip. "Some, possibly. I think the house was rented out for a while, so there were a lot of people who came and went within a short space of time. I'm not one of these nosy people who demand to know the ins and outs of everyone's business, am I, Sara?"

Sara shook her head. "I can vouch for that. Although Vera has been kind to us since we moved in, she waited until we approached her before she spoke to us. That was over a cup of milk, I seem to recall, wasn't it?"

"It was indeed. You felt you were failing Brian not offering him his cornflakes before he set off for work, I believe."

Sara blushed. "I like to take care of my man."

"That's commendable," Sally said, hopefully easing the woman's discomfort with a smile. "Are you up to giving us a statement, Sara? We'll need to get one each from you and your husband before the day is out."

"Okay. But I'm really not sure what else I can tell you other than what I've already said."

"That's all right. We just need to make things official. Sorry to have to ask you this, Vera, but would you mind if we do that here rather than drag Sara down the station with us?"

The older woman waved her hand in the air as if annoyed. "Get away with you. Of course I don't mind. I'd like to help if I can."

"Is there another room we can use? I hate to put you out like this."

"You're not. What about the kitchen? There's a table and chairs in there. Excuse the mess. I was about to start making a cake when Sara knocked on my door."

"Sorry," Sara apologised swiftly.

"Hush now, child. Forget I mentioned it. This is far more important than baking something that will only turn to fat."

Sally chuckled. The woman reminded her fondly of her own grandmother. "My gran used to say the same. It didn't stop her making dozens of cakes over the years, though."

"It's a bugger having a sweet tooth, but it's the only vice I have at my age. So why not indulge now and again? Do you want me to stay here, or should I go in the kitchen?"

"Perhaps Sara can go with Jack to go through her statement while I note down the names you can remember of the previous owners. How's that?"

Sara and Jack rose from their seats and left the room together. Sally could tell Sara was a little hesitant about what lay ahead by the speed she walked out of the room.

Sally withdrew her notebook from her pocket and smiled at Vera. "So, can you remember the date you bought the house, Vera?"

"I bought it in September of eighty-five. I remember it well because my daughter was born a few months after the move. My Ron —he died a couple of years back from a heart attack—was panicking because the sale took a while to go through. Damn solicitors, they do like to earn their money and hold things up when they can, don't they?"

"Any idea what the hold-up was, Vera?"

"A combination of things, really. The mortgage took a while to be approved because my hubby had not long changed his job. Then there was a problem with the boundary line that was highlighted by my solicitor. It all turned out well in the end. I seem to remember it took about four months to complete."

"That is a long time. It must have been frustrating for you."

"Very. Not only for me but for the woman and her family who were desperate to move out too."

Sally glanced up from taking her notes. "Desperate to move out? Can you tell me why?"

"I never did get to the bottom of why that was. Like I say, I'm not the inquisitive type. If people want to bare their soul to me, that's up to them. I'm not one for prying into people's business, though."

"I know it was a long time ago, but can you remember the woman's name?"

Vera pointed to her temple. "My hair might be grey, but there's nothing wrong with my brain, dear."

"I'm glad to hear that."

"Her name was Janet Ryland. She and her husband had three boys in their teens, I believe. What I can't remember are the boys' names, not that far back."

"That doesn't matter. We can delve into that when we get back to the station. I don't suppose you have a forwarding address for her?"

"Gosh, I used to because I forwarded a lot of post to her back in the day. Once the letters dried up for her, I'm afraid I threw her address away. Let me think for a moment, see if I can conjure it up for you." Vera stared at the flowered pattern in her carpet for a minute or two then shook her head. "I've failed. I'm sorry to let you down, dear."

"You haven't let me down. Far from it, in fact. I'm sure we'll be able to find her using the information you've already given me. Was she very old at the time?"

"Around thirty-five to forty, I'm guessing. She must have been to have had the teenage sons."

"Good detective work," Sally said, noting down the woman's observation.

"My old dad used to be a bobby on the beat years ago. I suppose I get those kinds of instincts from him. Lovely man, very strict in his manner. There was no messing about in his company, I can tell you. In those days, children were supposed to be seen and not heard, unlike the kids of today. I sit in my garden at times and pull my damn hair out. What is wrong with the children today? They're so vocal. They no longer speak to each other but shout at the top of their lungs. That is when they're not screaming or crying. And the bloody parents do little to try to dissuade them. Gosh, in my day, if my mother and father heard either me or my brother shouting in the street like an old fishwife, there would have been hell to pay. We would have been sent to our room and not allowed out for a month. The trouble with today's kids is that there is no discipline. Why is that, do you think, dear? Do you blame the schools for doing away with the cane or the slipper?" She waved her hand in front of her again. "Don't answer that. It was a rhetorical question."

"Hey, I agree with you wholeheartedly. Something has happened over the years, or not, as the case may be. I think the discipline side of things has wavered with most of today's parents. They seem to shove the kids out after school, not caring what they're up to. The amount of crimes that are reported because of youths misbehaving on the streets is multiplying every year. I fear we've gone off the track a little here. Going back to Janet Ryland, do you think her sons were well behaved?"

Vera shook her head. "Now that I couldn't tell you. We viewed the house several times before we bought it, but the lads were absent every time we came. She kept the house spick-and-span, so I'm thinking they were out a lot of the time, from under her feet. Don't quote me on that one. It's pure speculation on my part. I wouldn't have bought the house if it was a tip, I can tell you. People took pride in their homes in those days." Vera glanced out the window at the small terraced property across the street then pointed. "Look at that. A couple of old rusty cars on the drive and kids' toys strewn across the front garden. That family drive me to distraction with their lack of discipline for their three kids. They're only young. The oldest is probably seven, with the lungs of a professional opera singer. Awful, it is. If I were younger, I'd sell up in an instant. The trouble is, I wouldn't know where to begin with any of that. My Ron used to see to that side of things in the past." Her watery gaze drifted back to Sally. "I don't suppose you could have a quick word with them before you leave?"

"I will if you want me to. However, I wouldn't want any recriminations landing on your doorstep after I've gone."

Vera shook her head. "Is that what it has come to these days? Even the coppers are too worried about upsetting people for fear of what they might do in return?"

Sally dropped her chin to her chest. She was embarrassed to admit what she was about to say next. "I'm afraid it has. I do my bit where I can, but one word of complaint to some folks is like a red rag to a bull. My mum and dad went through hell a few years back. They own their house outright, but the houses opposite them are council-owned. A new family moved in and made my parents' lives hell. Loud music playing at all hours. Motorbikes and cars revving their engines and even racing in the street. My dad confronted the family one day, and things got considerably worse before I intervened and spoke to someone I knew at the council. The family were moved a few months later, but they made Mum's and Dad's lives tough right up until the day they left."

"At least you managed to get rid of the yobs and their loutish behaviour in the end."

"I did. But I know Mum and Dad still live on tenterhooks at times in case the family ever take umbrage and return. I installed a CCTV camera at the house for their peace of mind. It seems to have done the trick." That wasn't the prime reason Sally had installed the camera. She had moved back home around that time, and Darryl had sent a prison mate of his to damage her car. He'd even targeted her dog, Dex. Thankfully, the camera had caught him in the act.

"You seem a good daughter to your parents, love. I take my hat off to you."

"They're all I've got in this world, apart from my fiancé. Luckily, they all get on famously together. Dad and Simon are even set up in business together." Sally couldn't believe how relaxed and open she was being with the woman. It was totally out of character for her. She was usually a very private person on the quiet.

"That's nice when people get on so well like that. I do my best to get on with the neighbours. Sara and Brian are a really nice couple. I feel so bad that this has happened to them. I hope they don't end up leaving the house now."

"Maybe Sara will reconsider if nothing bad shows up on the inside of the house. Perhaps she'll be able to live with the fact that a body was buried in her back garden after all."

Vera inclined her head. "Would you?"

The woman had a point, and Sally was unsure how to answer her for a moment or two. "Okay, I'll admit I don't think I would be able to live here, knowing that. What were the neighbours before them like?"

"The one who sold the house to Sara and Brian? Well, David Pollett travelled around the country as a salesman. I used to keep an eye on the property during the week while he was away—only from a distance, that is. I was sad to see him move, but he decided to go and live up in Scotland. I think his firm gave him a new area to cover up there and promoted him to area manager at the same time. I was thrilled for him. Such a nice man, he was." Vera stood and crossed the room to a small mahogany bureau in the corner. She opened a drawer, extracted a small address book and returned to her seat. "Now, I know I have a forwarding address for him as we promised to send each other a card at Christmas."

Sally's spirits rose. "Excellent news. The more information you can share with us will make our job so much easier in the long run."

"Here it is." Vera passed the book over to Sally so she could jot down the address.

"Crikey, he's way up in the Highlands. Not sure I can afford the time off work to pay him a visit. I'll get the local police to go and see him. He lived next door for how long?"

Vera frowned a little. "About five years, I think."

"And before he arrived?"

"Well, that would have been my dear friend May Childs. She lived there for over forty years. Loved that house, she did. Died there in her sleep one day. Unfortunately, I was the one who found her. I had a key, you see. They all must trust me because they all ensure I have a key to the place. Anyway, I hadn't seen her around for a day or two, thought she'd gone off to visit a relative without telling me, so I let myself in and made sure the house was all safely locked up. I found her lying in her bed. She seemed so peaceful. Broke my heart at the time, it did. We were extremely close. She died of natural causes, the post-mortem said. Her heart simply gave out."

"Was she very old?"

"No more than sixty-five. No age really, not by today's standards, is it?"

"I suppose you're right. That's so sad."

"David was aware that May passed away in the house, but he didn't seem to mind. They were both lovely people, and I miss them both very much. Sara is a treasure, though. Again, we've hit it off right away, although she works odd shifts. She's a nurse at the hospital and tends to do the night shift most of the time. She's got the week off this week. That's why they started doing the work on the garden. I bet she regrets doing that now. Poor lass."

"Very unfortunate incident, one that will take time to get over, I'm sure. Going back to May Childs, Vera, was she married?"

"No, she refused several offers over the years. Always told me that she was determined to remain a spinster all her life as she preferred a peaceful existence. All the relationships she'd had before, she described as being 'volatile in nature'. She was such a gentle soul. Hard to believe someone of her demeanour could bring out the vile temper in some men. She went on the occasional date with a man, but as soon as the mask slipped and his true colours showed, she ditched him."

Sally nodded. After living with someone whose gentle nature had disguised the true monster buried beneath, she understood. "I see. Did all the men accept being ditched?"

Vera pondered the question for a few moments. "As far as I know, yes. Back in the day, you never heard about women being stalked by aggrieved men they had dumped, not like nowadays. The paper is full of women who have been stalked and badly beaten by their exes. No doubt you've had to deal with a few cases along those lines over the years, right?"

"I have." *Both professionally and personally, unfortunately.* "It appears to be an increasing trend, especially among the famous people, too. It's a strange and often terrifying world we live in due to the social media aspect of our lives."

"I hear that a lot. Whoever invented the internet and that damn Facebook has a lot to answer for, don't they? Yes, it's good for looking up things, but there's a dark side I keep hearing about that really ticks me off." Vera shuddered. "It doesn't bear thinking about at times. I'm glad I'm not younger and reliant on the internet to get my kicks."

Sally smiled. "Like you say, there are definite positives and negatives to using the internet. I must confess from a copper's point of view we find it invaluable most of the time. The amount of crimes I used to solve in my former role as a murder squad detective where a person's Facebook account revealed so much about the way they live their lives is nobody's business. Now I'm working as a cold case detective, I'm forced to go about solving the case the old-fashioned way. Mostly by legwork and talking to people such as yourself. We're superefficient at it, though—at least we have been in the past year since the team was created."

"That's wonderful. I remember when my father successfully solved a case, he used to be on a high for months back then."

Sally smiled. "Times have changed considerably since your father's day, I'm afraid. Because of the targets we're forced to meet monthly, we solve one case and immediately get started on the next. Last year, my team were given one hundred and ten cold cases to reinvestigate because of a technicality that showed up at head office. We're still trawling through those cases today, as well as having to deal with new cases that arise such as this one."

"Oh my goodness. That's horrendous," Vera said, looking genuinely appalled.

Sally shrugged. "It is what it is with modern-day policing."

Jack appeared in the doorway. "Can I have a quick word, boss, please?"

"Excuse me, Vera." Sally followed him out into the hallway. "What's wrong?"

He lowered his voice. "Nothing. I've got all I'm going to get out of her, I reckon. I think she's had enough right now and is asking me to call her husband."

"Understandable. They're both innocent in this, Jack. Let's not be too down on her for being affected by this. We need to take a statement from the husband, too, anyway."

"If he's going to tell us the same thing, perhaps we shouldn't call him home from work. I was thinking of sending a uniformed copper over to see him later."

"Makes sense to me. The couple will need to find other accommodation for the next few days while SOCO go through the house. Maybe you can arrange for them to stay elsewhere for me, too. I shouldn't be too long with Vera."

"Okay, I'll get on it now."

Sally returned to the lounge to find Vera standing by the window, observing her front garden, where the roses were about to bloom. "Are you all right, Vera?"

The woman turned to face her slowly. "I suppose it's only just sinking in now. The fact that a body has been buried next door all those years, and no one knew about it. I dread to think what that person's family went through if they went missing. What possesses someone to bury a body in a back garden like that? They can't possibly have an ounce of decency running through them, can they?"

Sally nodded. "I'm inclined to agree with you on that count. No one in their right mind would do such a thing. It's up to us to figure out who carried out the gruesome deed and why they felt the need to dispose of the body in such a shameful way. Everyone deserves a proper burial in this life. Of course, we'll ensure that happens now that the victim has been discovered. First, we have to go through the onerous task of finding out who the victim is. I have a feeling that's going to be difficult."

"I feel for you as well as that poor person's family. Mind you, if the person has been missing this long, I'm sure once they learn the body has been discovered, it will be a relief to them. That is if the relatives are still alive. Who knows about that?"

"Agreed. I can see this case will be fraught with many journeys going down avenues that will be closed to us just because of the timescale involved."

"I don't envy you one bit. I only hope that what I've managed to remember will help you solve the case and lead you to that poor person's family."

"I have no doubt about that. My partner is organising a few things for Sara, such as accommodation for the next few days. Once he's done that, we'll head back to the station to begin our investigation in earnest."

"I haven't given you much to go on, lovey, but it was the best I could come up with under the circumstances. Something might crop up in this old mind of mine later. If it does, I'll be sure to ring you."

Sally extracted a card from her pocket and gave it to Vera. "Ring me if you either think of anything or if something ends up concerning you about the case."

Vera walked towards the sofa and placed the card on the coffee table. "I'll be sure to do that. Is Sara all right?"

"She's struggling, I think. I'm sure I'd be the same if something like this had shown up on my doorstep. My partner is contacting her husband now."

"They're good people, Inspector. I'll be sure to support them in any way I can. They're welcome to stay with me for a few days. I'll suggest it to Sara, but I'm thinking she'll want to be as far away from here as possible."

Sara walked into the room and heard the tail end of the conversation. "You're exceptionally kind, Vera. I just wouldn't be able to sleep at night if I stayed around here a moment longer. I think I'm going to stay with Mum for a few days until things die down...oh dear, did I really say that?" she said, shaking her head regretfully.

"Don't worry about a slip of the tongue. It happens to the best of us at times."

Jack entered the room. "Sara, I've rung your husband. He's going to try and get home just after lunch, once he's organised his day around a little. I've made arrangements for an officer to go to his place of work to take down his statement, and I've also sorted out a double room for you at a local hotel. Do you know the Dolphin Hotel? It's the closest one I could find that had any vacancies, what with the bank holiday coming up."

"You're very kind. I think I know it. Would it be possible for me to pack a bag for Brian and myself?"

Jack looked over at Sally, who nodded. "We can arrange for someone to accompany you inside the house. There's no problem with that, Sara."

"Thank you. I assure you, it will be a case of shoving any necessary items in a few bags and getting out of there as fast as I can. When do you think we'll get the house back? Not that I ever want to step foot inside the place again. I intend putting it on the market as soon as possible." She sighed heavily. "I doubt anyone will want to buy it after this, though, right?"

"I can't deny that I think you're right thinking along those lines. Hopefully, I'm wrong about that."

"Oh dear, I know I'm coming across as being selfish when I should be thinking about that poor person and what their family must have gone through over the years. However, all our money is tied up in that house." She covered her face and sobbed.

Vera stepped forward and gathered Sara in her arms. "There, there, dear. I'm sure it will all turn out for the best eventually."

"I hope you're right," Sara muttered between sobs.

Sally's heart went out to the woman. She wouldn't know what to do if the same thing ever happened to her. So many people stretched themselves to buy their ideal home. To have something as devastating as a dead body show up in the back garden would knock anyone for six.

"One last thing before we leave you ladies. Sara, can you give me the name of your solicitor, please?"

"Of course. Let me think… It's Mitchell and Thomas Solicitors in Norwich."

"That's brilliant. We'll be in touch if we need to ask any further questions. Jack, have you taken down Sara's mobile number?"

He nodded. "All done."

"Excellent. Well, it was nice to meet you both. Sorry it had to be under such dire circumstances."

"Good luck," both ladies replied in unison.

Outside, Sally arranged for a female uniformed officer to accompany Sara into her home. Then she and Jack returned to the car and drove back to the station.

"How did it go with the old lady?" Jack asked once they were en route.

"She was extremely helpful with regards to telling me who the neighbours were over the years. Her father used to be a copper many moons ago, which probably helped."

"Interesting. Could she name any likely victims?"

"Nope. I know usually we'd go down the press conference route, however, that will have to wait for the time being until Simon comes up with some definitive details for us. Such as possible time of death and how old the victim was, of course."

"Should prove to be an interesting case if any evidence shows up."

Sally nodded. "Although it's a cold case, I don't think it can be treated that way just yet. We'll get Joanna searching the archives when we get back, see what surfaces there."

"What do you want me to do?"

"Let me get on to the solicitor first. Ask them to fax us the deeds to the house before we go any further. Then we'll all knuckle down to try to locate the ex-property owners. I have a feeling this is going to be a tricky case to solve. We need to prepare for that."

"Is there such a thing as an easy case to solve?"

Sally sniggered. "All right, you've got me there."

CHAPTER 3

BY MID-AFTERNOON, Sally and her team had the deeds to the property in their hands and the investigation was well underway. Joanna had worked her magic looking through the archives and made a startling discovery that would be foolish to ignore.

She called Sally over to her desk to run through what she'd uncovered. "You might want to take a seat, boss."

Sally pulled up a chair alongside her and leaned forward on the desk to peer at the screen. "What have you found out?"

Joanna brought up an article in the newspaper archives she was trawling through. "This. A Jeff Ryland was reported as missing back in nineteen eighty-five. His family address was the house next door, where Vera Harris now lives."

Sally sat back in her chair and whistled. "Wow, okay. Print off the article for me to read then try and track down the details of the original investigation. I think you've stumbled upon something here."

Joanna nodded and pressed a button on her keyboard. The printer churned out five sheets of paper, which she handed to Sally. On the top sheet was the image of a schoolboy taken in his school uniform. At first glance, he appeared to be a gentle character with smiling eyes.

Sally's heart constricted a little, and a small lump lodged itself in her throat as she read the article through to the end.

"Oh my. In one respect, I hope it is him, if only to give the family some closure, but heck, after all these years, this is going to come as devastating news if it does turn out to be Jeff Ryland. We need to try to find out where the family are now, if they've remained in the area or if they're still alive."

"I've got the original case file here, boss. The investigation was closed after ten years," Joanna said.

Jack glanced up from his desk. "So, we're dealing with a genuine cold case, after all, if he turns out to be the victim."

Sally's mind felt as though a tornado had found its way in through her ear. It was spinning off in different directions, confusing matters. She raised a hand. "Okay, we're talking purely speculation at this point. I'd rather not go steaming ahead just yet, not until Simon has given us something definite to go on. I'm going to give him a ring, let him know what we've discovered." Still in a state of semi-shock, she retired to her office with the article and placed the call. "Hi, Simon. Sorry to rush you, but do you have anything for me yet?"

"Hi. Why the eagerness on your part?"

"I spent the morning with the homeowner and the next-door neighbour, then we came back to the station and began digging."

"Where's this leading, Sal? Are you telling me you think you know who the victim is?"

"Sort of. We searched the database for any reports of people going missing around that time and discovered the neighbours' lad went missing in nineteen eighty-five. I've got the newspaper article in front of me that corroborates the story, plus my team have located the original investigation notes. The case was closed ten years later with the boy still missing."

"Boy? What age?"

"The reports say he was twelve. Why?"

"Well, it's far too early to confirm yet, but I've found a femur of a young person. If you pushed me to reveal what age I suspected the person it belongs to was, I would put them around the eleven-to-thirteen mark."

"Wow! That's amazing! So we could be onto something then, right?"

"Sally, rein yourself in a little. I need to ensure I'm right before I can give you the go-ahead. Please remember that."

"Okay, so how long are we talking here?" She tapped her pen on her desk as her impatience rose to a higher level.

"Another couple of days at least. I would suggest you go with your instinct and examine the missing boy's disappearance from a distance. Don't be too rash in reaching out to the family for now. Not until I can firm things up at my end."

"I hear you. It's got to be him, though, right? Logic tells you that it must be him."

"In your mind, perhaps. We all know how dangerous it can be forging ahead with a case when the proper evidence isn't in place. You'll have to excuse me. I have to get back to it now. You caught me having a sneaky coffee while I made some important calls regarding the last PM I completed."

"All right, you win. Consider me reining myself in. I'll see you later. Fancy going out for a meal tonight, or shall I order a takeaway?"

"Let's go down the takeaway route for now."

"Okay, love you."

Simon sniggered and hung up. It was unusual for Sally to show any affection towards him while she was at work, but something about this case had already brought out an emotional side in her that she was finding difficult to suppress. She studied the boy's photo again and shook her head. She'd only dealt with a few child murder cases throughout her career, and despite her never wanting children of her own, she couldn't help but be affected when such a case crossed her desk. Maybe it was their short lifespans that affected her the most. She couldn't put her finger on what else it could likely be that churned up her insides and messed with her head.

Feeling a little maudlin, she reached for the phone and rang her mother. "Hey, Mum. How are things there?"

"Hello, love. To what do I owe the pleasure? It's rare for you to ring during your working day. Is everything all right?"

She sighed. "Yes and no. Oh, ignore me. How's Dex?"

"Missing you, as always. I can barely drag him away from the hallway. He lies there all day, waiting for you to walk through the door. I don't think I've ever come across a more devoted dog before in my life."

"Oh, Mum, now the guilt has truly set in, as well. Will you give him a hug from me?"

"As well? Of course I'll give him a hug. Come on, love, what's wrong? If I can help, you know I'll do my best."

"You can't, Mum. No one can help. I'm feeling a tad emotional today, that's all. Nothing a call home won't cure."

"Why? There must be a reason, darling. Talk to me."

"A new case has sprung up that involves a child. You know how much they affect me, lord knows why."

"Oh dear, that's not good. My heart goes out to you, sweetheart. You've done the right thing ringing me if it helps you come to terms with your emotions faster. Best to have a good cry and get it out of your system. It works every time for me."

Sally chuckled. "I don't think it has quite come to that yet, Mum. How's Dad?"

"Improving daily. He's at the auction house now, in fact. Considering the next bargain for the business. He was driving me nuts being under my feet all day. The doctor gave him the all-clear to start work again last week, and he was chomping at the bit to get to the auction again. I offered to go with him, but he virtually snapped my head off. Said that I wasn't to overprotect him and that he had to face getting back to work eventually."

"He's strong-willed. You know that, Mum. I doubt he'll encounter any problems in the future. If he does, let me know, and I'll intervene like last time."

"Who knows when these morons will emerge, love? The attack he suffered was all about the money aspect. People are out to make a quick profit nowadays. Some more determined than others to fulfil their greed. Anyway, you know what your father's like once he has his eye set on something."

"I do. I'm sure that's the end of the trouble for him now, Mum. Simon is really excited at the prospect of Dad returning to work again. He's eager to add to their portfolio of properties—if there are any bargains still around to be had, that is. There seems to be so many people searching for derelict or unloved properties to renovate currently."

"I hear you, love. But you're always going to get a gem coming on the market, mostly when an old relative dies and leaves a run-down house in their estate."

"That's true. Okay, time's marching on. Give my love to Dad when he comes home. Don't hesitate to ring me if you have any concerns about him. Promise?"

"We'll be fine, love. Will you and Simon be coming for Sunday dinner, as usual?"

"We'd love to, Mum. See you at the normal time. Love you lots, and thanks for the chat to help put life back in perspective once again."

"Have a good day, love."

"You, too, Mum." Sally ended the call and replaced the phone in the docking station. Then she left her seat and walked over to the window to admire the flat landscape of the Norfolk countryside beyond. She often did this when she needed to clear her mind. After a few moments, everything seemed a lot clearer. She opened the door and stepped into the incident room with a renewed vigour.

She made her way over to the whiteboard and noted down all the information they had managed to gather so far. Using her notebook as guidance for the dates, she placed the names of the people who owned the house in chronological order. Beside each name, she jotted down a few questions that were puzzling her. Alongside May Childs, she added, *did May have any family in the area? Who inherited the property? Did they sell it immediately?* She also wrote down Vera Harris's name and some of the pertinent information she had supplied. Then she added David Pollett's name, with a note alongside saying to contact him only if clues dried up elsewhere as nothing so far seemed to fit with his time at the house.

Finally, she capitalised the name JANET RYLAND, and in the centre of the board, she wrote her son's name in capital letters and circled it a few times. She turned to her team and asked, "What do we have on the Rylands?"

Joanna raised her head. "I'm in the process of trying to locate them all now, boss. I think I've managed to find the mother's address via the electoral roll, but I'd like to check that before I hand it over."

"I trust your judgement on that, Joanna. Jack, any news from the solicitor on the deeds front? Just in case Vera's memory wasn't up to scratch and she missed a proprietor out."

"The solicitor was with a client. I told his PA what information I needed, and she promised to fax through the details before the end of the day."

"Good. What else do we have?" she asked, more to herself than the others as she faced the board once more. "Ah yes, just a heads-up for you all—when I spoke to Simon, he roughly confirmed that the bones were indeed that of a child between the ages of eleven and thirteen, but that was off the record until he has carried out his extensive examination. At this moment, I wouldn't want to be in his shoes for all the poppy fields in Afghanistan."

"What?" Jack queried.

Sally sniggered. "Well, everyone says all the tea in China. I was just trying to be clever in my own inimitable way."

"I have to tell you, boss, it didn't work."

Sally smiled at him. "Obviously."

The information the team needed to take things forward was slow to come in during the afternoon, and Sally became anxious. She turned to the files in her office to see if there was another case they could run alongside the other one rather than have lulls in their days where nothing was going to get done. She had a mantra in life that it was always better to be busy than to tap her feet waiting for the information to come.

She placed a couple of the files to one side that appeared to be less interesting and picked up one that angered her more than any other case she'd read lately. Christopher Abbott was sitting in prison after pleading guilty to murdering a ten-year-old child, Lynn Jackman. He'd been linked to several other crimes, but nothing definitive had come of the other cases. Over the years, Abbott had maintained a silence about where the bodies of a number of his suspected victims were buried. Numerous officers had tried to break him down, but he'd stood his ground and kept his mouth firmly closed.

The more she studied the file, the more something bugged her. *Bingo! That's it.* Sally nodded. "All the investigating officers were men. Maybe it's time a woman went to see him. Perhaps work on his compassionate side, if he has one." She scribbled down some notes about the case in her notebook then looked up the number they had on file for any of the relatives of Abbott's victims involved in the investigation. Sally rang one of the relatives whose daughter's body was still missing.

"Hello, is that Miranda Hathaway?"

"It is," the woman replied, a note of suspicion tinging her tone.

"Sorry to ring you out of the blue like this. I'm DI Sally Parker. I'm in charge of a relatively new cold case team that has been set up in the area."

The woman gasped. "Does this mean you're going to reopen Katrina's—my daughter's case?"

"As far as I'm concerned, her case was never closed. Not according to the file, anyway. I'm sorry no one has been in touch with you recently."

"You're not the only one. I need to know what happened to my baby before..." The woman broke off in a sob.

Sally's chest constricted a little in discomfort. "I'm sorry. The last thing I wanted to do was upset you. Before what, Mrs. Hathaway?"

After a long pause, during which the woman tried to compose herself, she mumbled, "Before I die. I have terminal cancer. The doctor has given me three months to live."

Sally closed her eyes, trying to force back the tears threatening to emerge. That was the problem with handling cold cases. Since the original crime was committed, the lives of those left behind could have changed dramatically.

"I'm so very sorry."

"There's no need for you to be sorry, Inspector. I've learnt to live with the prognosis and accepted my fate. What would be wonderful is me going to my grave knowing what happened to my baby and possibly laying her body to rest after all this time."

"I'll see what I can do. A word of caution if I may. Looking over the case file, it's going to take a massive effort, and I fear it's going to be exceedingly challenging to get Abbott to talk. I noticed one extraordinary fact that could work in our favour, though—over the years, none of the investigating officers were women."

"You're right. I hadn't thought about that before. Maybe you'll prove to be the good omen we need to find our daughter. To make things clear, I accepted her death long ago. I can feel her around me every day, so I know she's passed away. I'd appreciate knowing where he put her body, though. It's important for me to lay her body some-where sacred. Somewhere her brother and sister can visit to pay their respects."

"I totally understand that. I just wanted to contact you to make you aware of the situation. I have every intention of visiting Abbott in the next day or two. Of course, I'll keep you informed of any news that surfaces right away. Please, I wanted to assure you that I will do everything in my power to get the information from the prisoner."

"Thank you. I'll be sitting here, waiting for your call, Inspector, with everything crossed."

"I'll be in touch soon."

Sally left her office and returned to the incident room. She headed for the vending machine and bought all the team coffee, which she distributed. Stopping at Jack's desk, she sighed and sat in the chair next to him. "Anything?"

"Nope, it's a waiting game, as per usual. What have you been up to? Mindless paperwork?"

"Not exactly. Something made me look at the case files again, and I've extracted a case that I think we should prioritise."

Jack frowned and sat back in his chair. "Whoa! As well as this one?"

"Yes, Jack. Do you have a problem with that notion?"

"No." He pulled an imaginary zip across his lips.

She shook her head and smiled. "You know what I'm like. I get frustrated when a case proves to be slow to get off the ground. I need to be actively doing something. It makes sense to run the two cases alongside each other. Let's face it—this isn't the first time we've attempted to do it."

"I know. Hey, don't mind me. You're the boss. What you say goes, right?"

She furrowed her brow. "Do I sense a little reluctance?"

"Not at all. I hope it doesn't backfire and cause us to be over-whelmed. On your head be it."

"Thanks for the support, partner. You haven't even asked about the case. Aren't you curious?"

He stretched and yawned. "Go on then, surprise me."

"Does Christopher Abbott ring a bell?"

Jack thought it over for a moment then shook his head.

"Sorry to eavesdrop, boss. It does with me," Joanna said behind her.

Sally turned to face her. "You remember the case?"

"Yes. From when I was younger. I was still living at home at the time, and I recall the commotion going on at the end of my road when they arrested the man."

"Bloody hell, Joanna! I had no idea. So he lived in your street?"

"Not exactly. At the junction of our road. One of his victims lived in the same road. At the time of her death, my parents instructed me to give them my itinerary for every second of the day. They were super protective of me back then, even though I was nineteen. I have to admit that I tended not to go out at night much up until the time he was caught. As soon as my father realised what was going on, he marched down to the bottom of the road with our male neighbours and confronted Abbott when they put him in the back of the police car. The whole neighbourhood lived under a cloud for a few months. I recall there was an awful lot of guilt flying around between the neighbours."

"Guilt? Why guilt?" Sally asked, perplexed.

"Some people said they suspected something was going on in his house but never spoke up. A few of them admitted they saw several young women enter the house and never leave it."

"Oh crap. That's awful. Fancy living with that on your conscience. I just rang one of his suspected victims' mothers, a Miranda Hathaway."

"Mother of Katrina Hathaway, right?" Joanna asked.

"You're right. Did you know the girl?"

"She went to my school. She was in the year lower than me and lived a few streets away. Abbott is a vile son of a bitch, boss."

"Aren't they all?" she replied with a smile, hoping Joanna would get the inference to Darryl.

Joanna nodded, a sympathetic expression on her flushed face. "They are. What's going to be your first step? Do you want me to bring up the archives on the case?"

"Hang fire on that. I'd really like you to keep pressing on with finding the Ryland family, if you will. I'd like to tinker with this case on my own for now."

"No problem, boss. If I have a spare minute, I'll try and print the reports off in between."

Sally laughed. "I forgot how talented you were at multitasking. I'm not going to stop you, but please give priority at all times to the Ryland case."

"I will. I promise."

Sally turned her attention to Jack, enabling Joanna to get on with the tasks in hand relating to the Ryland case.

"Who'd have thunk it?" Jack whispered.

Sally rolled her eyes. "It's a small world. Too small, at times. Anyway, I'm going to pay Abbott a visit in prison."

"Want me to come with you?"

"I'm sure I'll be fine. I'll ring the governor in a moment and arrange a meeting with Abbott in the next day or two."

"Watch you don't burn yourself out. I have a feeling you're going to regret taking on another case once the information we need starts trickling through on this one."

"Hopefully, I'll be able to prove you wrong, matey. Anyway, there's an extra incentive for us to solve this one."

"What's that?"

"Miranda Hathaway is terminally ill."

Jack shook his head in despair. "Oh shit! That's a bummer. Okay, then I can understand you wanting to deal with this case. Promise me one thing."

"What's that?"

"That you ask for help if you need it and don't take your work home with you."

Sally chuckled. "Yes, boss. Just to put your mind at rest on that front, Simon would crucify me if I did that nowadays. We've made a pact to leave work behind us as soon as we step through the front door at night."

Jack raised a sceptical eyebrow. "And pray tell me how that's working out between the two of you?"

Sally pulled a face at him. "Hit and miss, but you knew that already."

"I thought as much. You need to chill more. There's such a thing as being too devoted to a job. You can't tell me the people at head office appreciate the amount of extra hours you put in."

"Probably not. Nevertheless, it makes me feel good, Jack. It's also very difficult changing a habit of a lifetime, too."

"Granted. Donna will back me up when I say that I leave my work behind me."

Sally laughed. "Now why doesn't that surprise me? Right, I'm going to make a call. Keep plodding on, gang." She left her seat and took her coffee back to her office. When she placed the call to the prison in Norwich, she found the governor to be friendly but officious.

"Would you grant me permission to come and visit Abbott, Mr. Ward?"

"Of course. Although it wouldn't be right of me not to try to dissuade you. He's a nasty piece of work, Inspector. Caused more problems on the inside than any other inmate here."

"I'm positive I can handle him. You'll ensure there's a prison guard with me when I interview him, I take it?"

"It would be mighty foolish of me not to guarantee that occurs. When are you thinking of coming?"

"Time's getting on now. By the time I drove out there, it would be around six. That wouldn't be good for you, would it?"

"You're right. Maybe leave it until the morning, in that case?"

Sally nodded, forgetting he couldn't see her. "Agreed. I can be there for ten thirty in the morning, if that suits you."

"It does. I'll see you then."

"Look forward to meeting you." She hung up. Mr. Ward was new to the job. He'd taken over from the governor who had been helpful in getting Darryl transferred to Scotland. The previous governor had retired in the last few months, according to the secretary who had patched her through to Mr. Ward.

The rest of the afternoon was spent nipping in and out of the incident room to check on the team's progress. In between, Sally opened the odd brown envelope to deal with. At six o'clock, she decided to call it a day and went into the outer office to dismiss the team. They all seemed a little dejected not to have discovered anything substantial. Sally assured them that things would look much brighter in the morning and told them to go home and have a rest.

She left the station with her partner. "Thanks for all your efforts today, Jack. It's appreciated, as always."

"There's no need to say that. We all know how much you appreciate us, even through the extremely frustrating times, like today."

"Maybe tomorrow will be different. Don't forget I'll be heading off for the prison first thing."

"Will you be going straight from home?"

"I might as well. You know how busy the roads leading into Norwich can be at that time of the morning."

"Yep. I'm surprised at you forgetting about that when you made the arrangements."

"I know. I'm such an idiot once my enthusiasm for a case takes over. Have a good evening. Send my regards to Donna and the kids."

"Will do. Drive carefully in the morning. There's no need for you to do your Lewis Hamilton impersonation on the open roads."

Sally roared with laughter. "As if I would." She jumped in the car and rang Simon's mobile. "Hey, how are you doing?"

"I'm packing up, getting ready to leave. Should be home in about half an hour. What about you?"

"I'm leaving now. Want me to pick up a Chinese on the way home?"

"You read my mind. I'll have a beef chop suey and fried rice. I'll pick up the tab for this one; you bought the last one we had."

"Don't worry. You can take me out for a slap-up meal at the weekend. See you soon."

She ended the call and drove to the smart Chinese restaurant just down the road from Simon's house. The food was the best she'd ever eaten whether it was at the table in the restaurant or as a takeaway meal.

Sally pulled into the drive and placed the key in the front door as Simon parked his car behind her. They shared a brief kiss then served up the meal before she divulged what Jack had jestingly suggested about Gretna Green earlier that day. "What do you think? I'd love all our friends to be at the wedding. Hate the thought of omitting anyone in case it causes ill-feeling in the future."

Simon chewed his lower lip for a few minutes before he finally grinned. "I think it's an excellent idea. Of course, we'd need to fork out for accommodation for everyone, too. We can't expect them to pay for that."

"Even if we do that, it's going to be a darn sight cheaper than an over-the-top wedding." She flung her arms around his neck and kissed him, tasting the saltiness lingering on his lips from the meal they had shared. "It's going to be a fabulous wedding. I can feel it in my bones."

"Now all we have to do is pick a date and hope that everyone will be able to attend. There's bound to be a couple who won't be able to make the trip."

"This is the most excited I've been for a long, long time. I'll see if I can squeeze in the time to ring the wedding planners up there and check what dates they have available. They'll probably be booked up for two years in advance, knowing our luck."

"Don't be such a pessimist. I'll ring them, if you like. You have enough on your plate at work at the moment, love."

"That's kind of you, Simon. You're a gem. I don't know how long I'm going to be stuck in Norwich tomorrow, so it might be best if you do it."

"Norwich? What's that about?"

She inhaled a deep breath then let it out slowly. "I have to question a prisoner."

Simon stiffened. "About what?"

"It's nothing to worry about. I know what's concerning you, and it's fine. I've rung the governor already, and he's assured me there will be a guard in the room with me during the visit. I'm not apprehensive about it in the least, love."

"Well, I am. Is Jack going with you?"

His face was stern. She wondered for the briefest of moments if she should lie. Nonetheless, she decided against it and shook her head. "No. It'll be fine, I promise."

"Why isn't he going with you?"

"Simon, please, this was my decision to go alone. I need Jack to concentrate on the other case we're dealing with. The Ryland case." She went on to explain the phone call she'd had with Miranda Hathaway, and he seemed far more willing to accept the situation. "I need to do this, if only for her sake, love. Don't be cross with me."

He grasped her hand in his. "I'm not angry. I apologise if it came across like that. I'm just concerned. You're soon going to be my wife. I suppose I'm being a tad selfish, not wanting anything harmful to happen to you. It's only because I care. Nothing more sinister than that, I promise."

"I know. Hey, I love you even more for caring so much about me." They shared a kiss again then cleared up the kitchen before they retired to bed for an early night.

CHAPTER 4

SALLY LEFT the house around nine the following morning, and it wasn't until she was ten minutes away from the prison that the butterflies took flight in her stomach. She decided to give herself a good talking to before she arrived. "Don't be foolish, girl. If you go in there looking scared shitless, he's going to mock you from the outset. Harden up!"

With her nerves still intact, only just, she parked the car and approached the visitors' entrance, withdrawing her warrant card from her pocket before she entered the building.

An officer in uniform greeted her with a brief nod. "Can I help?"

"I'm here to see one of the prisoners, Christopher Abbott. Governor Ward is aware of my visit."

"Ah yes, I have a note here to expect you. Empty your pockets then pass through the barrier, if you will?"

Sally did as she was instructed and sighed in relief when the alarm didn't go off. In her experience, the machines were hypersensitive, and it usually only took an innocent belt buckle or something similar to set off the alarm. She had dressed extra carefully that morning with that in mind.

The officer walked her through the gloomy narrow corridors, and the hairs on the back of her neck stood on end as thoughts of her last encounter with her ex sprang to mind. She tried to shove his image back in the little box where she usually stored it and quickly focussed on what lay ahead of her. She had a feeling she was going to need all her inner strength to deal with Abbott.

At the end of the second corridor, the officer stopped outside the governor's office and rapped his knuckles on the door. A voice bellowed an answer, instructing them to enter.

Sally followed the officer into the room. Governor Ward was in his fifties. Large-rimmed spectacles sat on his nose, and his hair was mostly a steely grey.

"Hello, Governor Ward. It's good to meet you."

He rose from his chair and invited her to take a seat. Extending his hand, he shook hers briefly. "The pleasure is all mine. You're a little early. Can I get you a drink?"

"Not for me, thank you. The traffic was better than anticipated."

"Not many people can say that at this time of the morning. Right, I've told the officers on his wing that you will be questioning Abbott today. No one foresees any problems, but as a precaution, two of the officers have volunteered to be on duty during your interview—one inside the room and the other standing guard outside."

Sally inclined her head. "If you think that's necessary."

"I do. I wouldn't feel I was doing my job properly if those men weren't in place. As I told you on the phone, the man has caused a lot of problems in here over the years. Some of those incidents have led to his time behind bars being increased. Some prisoners never learn."

"Has he ever spoken about his victims?"

"Not to me. I dug out his file yesterday after you rang me, and by all accounts, he's had numerous dealings with shrinks over the years. They've never once broken through his barriers, though. He's one of the most determined men I've ever had the misfortune of dealing with in my time in the prison service."

"Not what I wanted to hear, but thank you for the warning. Hopefully, I can change all that and make him open up to me."

"Good luck. I'll show you to the interview room myself, if you're ready?"

"I'm ready and more than willing," Sally replied as she left her chair and followed the governor out of the room.

She walked deeper into the bowels of the prison, her legs and shoulders stiffening with tension. Shaking her arms out relieved some of that stress, but a certain amount still lingered when the governor showed her into a small room and gestured for her to take a seat.

"I'll get my men to bring Abbott through. Good luck," Governor Ward said a second time.

During the wait, Sally busied herself by getting her notebook out and making a few notes in the likelihood that she forgot anything once the prisoner joined her. Within minutes, the door opened. She glanced up to see a man wearing jeans and a T-shirt. His gaze latched on to hers instantly. His eyes narrowed and widened a few times in a couple of seconds and his gaze intensified, not only taking in her facial features, but travelling down the length of her body also.

The prison officer accompanying him gave him a slight shove, enough to get him moving again. "In you go, Abbott."

Abbott entered the room, shuffling due to the chains around his ankles. Sally held the man's gaze as he walked. The officer pulled out the chair on the other side of the table and ordered Abbott to sit.

With a humph, he fell into the chair. He placed his cuffed hands on the table and twirled his thumbs around each other. "It's about time they sent someone pretty to see me."

"Keep it respectful, Abbott," the officer warned from his position behind Abbott's chair.

"Hello, Christopher. Is it all right if I call you that?"

His right shoulder hitched up then dropped. "Why not? And you are?"

"Detective Inspector Sally Parker."

His head tilted, and a glimmer of a smile inched his lips apart. "An inspector, eh? So, they finally decided to send in the big boys …oops, I mean big girls, in your instance."

"I've been put in charge of a cold case team, and your file ended up on my desk."

His chained hands flew up to his chest, and his eyes glistened with excitement. "I'm innocent. I've been telling these clowns that for years, and no one has listened to me. Thank you for finally believing me, Inspector."

Sally shook her head. "The evidence proves otherwise, as you know well."

He roared and tipped his head back. "It was worth a try. Good to see my acting skills are still on the mark."

"You didn't fool me, Christopher. I've met your type dozens of times over the years."

"You have? How many years would that be, Sally?"

The sound of her name rolling off his tongue made her skin crawl. She dug deep, refusing to reveal the effect he was having on her. "Too many to mention," she replied evasively.

"Why the secrecy? All I'll do when you've gone is Google you."

"That's your prerogative. Depending on how this interview pans out, I could always ask the governor to withhold your privileges."

The officer behind Abbott's chair cleared his throat. "He doesn't have those kinds of privileges, Inspector. He's winding you up."

Sally nodded at the officer. "Thank you for that." She then asked Abbott, "Why lie? Where do these lies get you in the end?"

"Extra time in here."

The man's blasé attitude got to her. He had no right to be so nonchalant after all these years of being locked up. Where was the remorse he should have been riddled with? "You must like it in prison, Christopher. Is that what you're saying?"

"Read into my remark what you will, Sally."

"Don't you want to revert back to living a normal life after years of being locked up?"

"Not really. I get fed and watered in here at the tax payers' expense. Even get a bit of pocket money when I'm a good boy." He grinned, showing off his gleaming white teeth.

"You do? I hear your time behind bars has been lengthened due to your bad behaviour."

"You're well informed, Sally. Maybe I misbehave because I know where it will lead. Perhaps I have every intention of staying in here until the day I die."

"May I ask why you would want to give up on your freedom like that?"

"Does there always have to be a reason in this life?"

Sally's eyes narrowed. "What are you afraid of? The families seeking their revenge?"

He laughed and tipped his head back again. "Nope. Next scenario!"

"Have you ever felt remorse for your actions, Christopher?" She used his name regularly, trying to desensitise the man.

His hands rose to his chin, and he rubbed a finger and thumb around his day-old stubble as he contemplated her question for a few minutes. When it came, his answer was brief and to the point. "No."

Sally inhaled a deep breath. He was going to be a tough cookie to crack. "That's a shame. Don't you think the parents of the missing girls deserve to know where their daughters are?"

"Nope."

"Put yourself in their shoes. What if a member of your family had gone missing and was presumed dead for years? Wouldn't you want to learn the truth?"

His mouth turned down at the sides, and he shook his head. "Nope. It wouldn't interest me one iota. There is something that might change my mind, though."

Her hopes spiked. "There is? What's that?"

"If you were to bring me photos."

"Photos? Of what? The victims?"

He nodded slowly as if to emphasise his point. "The victims that were found. I want to see their bodies. More importantly, the crime scene photos."

"What? Why?" Sally was appalled by the eagerness that had risen in the man's demeanour.

His lips parted and spread into an ever-widening smile. "I miss them. I want to be reunited with them."

Sally was taken aback by his warped honesty. "How many did you kill?"

"How many does it say on my file again?"

"Six. Three bodies have been discovered so far over the years."

He raised his eyebrows and dropped them a few times, still grinning like a deranged clown. "Then six it is."

"Are you telling me there were more?"

"You're the detective, Sally. What do you think?"

"I think you're making it up just to get me going."

"What could I possibly achieve by doing that?"

Sally glared at him. "It's all about the mind games with you, isn't it? That's the challenge for you now that you're unable to get your hands on another victim."

He shrugged. "It was never about the sex with the girls. I told the arresting no-mark officer that at the time. It's not my fault he chose to disbelieve me. The girls had sex with me of their own free will. I never forced myself upon them at any time. It was their brains that stimulated me the most. All the girls I abducted were well educated and could hold an intelligent conversation when the need arose."

"So why kill them?"

"Once they started whining that they wanted to go home, I grew bored with them and moved on to the next girl immediately."

Sally ran through the man's file in her mind. She focussed on the date each girl went missing and realised there were inconsistencies. "Okay, so that means you abducted ten girls in total."

He inclined his head and nodded. "You're good. I'll give you that. Of course, I'm neither denying nor admitting to any further crimes."

"You don't have to. I've worked it out for myself. Where are the girls buried?"

His cuffs jangled as he raised his hands and placed a finger on his cheek. "Let me see now. Oh yes, you might want to take notes here, Inspector." He paused until Sally had hurriedly opened her notebook to a fresh page. "The first one was buried at..."

Sally raised her head to look at him. His eyes glistened with amusement. "You're not going to tell me, are you?"

"Nope. Where would be the fun in that?"

Sally flipped her notebook shut again. "You make me sick."

"You're not the first to utter those words, and I doubt you'll be the last, either."

"Just tell me how many? Was I right thinking there were ten girls?"

"You might have been."

Sally heaved out a large sigh. She had only one card left to lay on the table. "Okay, do you want to know the real reason I've come to see you today?"

"I'm intrigued. Of course I am. No one from your mob has visited me in years. What's altered?"

Sweat broke out on her brow, and the palms of her hands became sticky under his watchful gaze. "I need to know where you disposed of Katrina Hathaway's body."

"Why? Why her, and why now?" His eyes narrowed.

Sally dropped her gaze to the table then raised it to meet his again. "Because her mother has terminal cancer, and she's desperate to bury her daughter before she loses her own life."

"That's a shame. Just think, she'll soon be reunited with her again when her time comes."

"Do you have no compassion?"

He shook his head. "Very little. It's not something that was instilled in me as a child. Do you want to talk about what I went through as a kid?"

"If it will help, then by all means, tell me." She watched the changing emotions cross his face and, for once, felt as if she might be making some progress with him.

"It all started when I was four. My whore of a mother took me into her bed and raped me. She laughed all the way through the vile encounter... You don't seem shocked by that revelation, Sally."

"Over the years, I've dealt with many serial killers who have recounted a similar experience."

"And have you shown your compassionate side when that has happened?"

"No. I couldn't. Every single person on this earth has had the misfortune to suffer at the hands of others at one time in their life. Not everyone chooses to let such vile events affect their future."

"Interesting take on things. So, what's been your bad experience in this world, DI Sally Parker?"

She shuffled in her chair for a few moments before finding her voice. "Having the misfortune to deal with people as bad as you."

"Is that it? Because I can see in your eyes that you're telling me a lie. Be honest with me."

Sally slowly shook her head. "I guess we're somewhat at an impasse then. I'll reveal the truth when you tell me where you've buried the girls."

"I admire your persistence, Sally. Even though it's a little misguided. I have the power, yet you continue to take me for a fool."

"You think it's *power* you hold? I call it vindictiveness. These families have the right to know where their kin are buried."

"Who's saying they're all dead? Maybe a few of them pleaded with me to give them money so they could escape the confines of their family home."

"Is that true?"

He shrugged. "You should ask the families what type of relationship they had with their daughters and go from there. You're not stupid, Sally. You can see through people if you really dig deep enough."

"I'll look into it. One last time before I leave. Please, I'm begging you. At least tell me where you've buried Katrina Hathaway, for her mother's sake?"

He glared at her. "What if she was one of the girls I was referring to, who pleaded with me to help her get away from her family?"

Sally rose from her chair, surprising Abbott. "I don't believe you."

His cuffed hands reached out to her. "Wait! I'll do a deal with you. Bring me the crime scene photos from the three girls you found, and I'll tell you where she's buried."

"Are you telling me that she *is* dead?"

His gaze dropped to the table, his eyes finally breaking contact with hers. He'd slipped up, and he knew it.

Her voice softened when she pleaded, "Do the right thing for once in your life. Don't you think Miranda and the other parents have suffered enough over the years? What do you hope to accomplish by not revealing the truth?"

When his eyes met hers again, a strange malevolence had appeared in their depths. "Officer, I'm ready to go back to my cell now. We're done here."

The officer shrugged when Sally glanced at him as he helped Abbott to his feet. The prisoner swivelled sideways and shuffled away from her.

"Please, wait! Don't go yet. I have more questions that need answering."

"Next time…when you bring the photos."

Dumbfounded, Sally watched the officer escort him from the room. She'd got so much out of him during the interview, yet so little.

How can that be? He's got me by the short and curlies.

The prison officer who had been on guard outside the room poked his head around the door. "Are you ready to go?"

Reluctantly, she pushed back her chair and stood. After gathering her notebook and pen, she followed the officer through the hallways and back to the governor's office to apprise him briefly of how the interview had gone. With the governor brought up to date, she returned to her car and drove back to the station. During the journey, she replayed her time with Abbott and the lost opportunity.

CHAPTER 5

THE TEAM all turned her way when she entered the incident room.

"Well?" Jack urged before she'd barely taken a few steps.

"Give me a chance, partner. Better still, you could welcome me back with a cup of coffee. I clearly haven't trained you well enough over the years."

Jack mumbled a complaint under his breath and sprang to his feet. Sally winked at Joanna and pulled out a chair close to Jack's desk. He returned with the coffee and placed it grudgingly in front of her.

"Well?" he repeated, falling into his chair.

"Well, that was an experience and a half. One that I'd rather not have to repeat anytime soon. Except I'm going to have to."

"Do you have to be so cryptic with your answers all the time?" Jack demanded impatiently.

Sally laughed. "Hardly *all* the time, partner. What's rattled your cage while I've been out?"

"Nothing. Will you please tell us what went on during your visit?"

Sally rolled her eyes, took a sip of coffee and exhaled a large breath. "Apart from him hinting there are more bodies out there than the original inquiry suggested…"

"What? He told you that?"

"No, he didn't openly come out and say it. He stated that once he got rid of one girl, he abducted another one virtually straight away. I need to check the timelines of when the girls were reported missing to corroborate what he said. However, most of the dates stuck in my head, and I tackled him about the gaps that leapt to mind. I'm thinking he murdered in the region of ten girls as opposed to the six he was charged for, but that's going to take a lot of delving into. Jordan, do you want to work with me on this one?"

Jordan glanced up from the notes he was taking at his desk and nodded. "Sounds like an intriguing case, boss. I'd love to work on it."

"Okay, I'm going to need you to trawl back through the archives around the time of the other girls' deaths and reports of when they went missing. Try and match up any gaps with any possible missing person reports at that time in the same area."

"Will do. How far do you want me to extend the area to?"

"Again, go by what we know with the other girls' locations and make the judgement call yourself. I wouldn't go farther afield than say ten or fifteen miles, if I were you."

"Leave it with me. I'll get back to you as soon as I find anything significant."

"Good man." She turned back to Jack and asked, "What have you guys managed to find out in my absence this morning?"

"Joanna has worked wonders. You tell her, Joanna."

"I've been trying to track down the names on the list, boss, and I have some good news about the mother of Jeff Ryland."

Sally eagerly sat forward in her chair. "You have? What's that?"

"She's still alive. Now living just over the border in Suffolk, not too far."

"I don't blame her selling up. Any idea when she moved out of the area?"

"When she sold the house to Vera Harris. Soon after she reported her son missing."

Sally frowned. "How strange. It's definitely not something I would do in the circumstances. Would any of you?"

There was a collective shake of the head as she glanced around the team.

"Maybe the trauma of waiting for the doorbell to ring with news grew too much for her," Jack chipped in.

"Maybe. Then why didn't she inform us? Perhaps she did, and someone neglected to update the file. What a cock-up!"

"Hey, I guess we've got to be thankful that she's still alive after all these years. It doesn't always turn out that way."

"Where exactly does she live, Joanna?"

"On the coast at Lowestoft."

Sally nodded and worked out the distance in her mind. "What's that? About an hour's run from here, Jack?"

"Give or take five minutes, I'd say. What are you thinking?"

"That I should drink this quickly, and we should pay her a visit before the news breaks on TV."

"But the body hasn't formerly been identified as yet. Are you truly willing to put her through all that trauma, boss?"

"It's a difficult one, granted. But looking at things from her perspective, I'd want to know as soon as there was any kind of news, wouldn't you?"

Jack hitched up his shoulders and dropped them again. "I guess so. Maybe you should ring your old man first, see how things are progressing there before we jump in with both feet."

Sally widened her eyes. "My old man? Are you referring to my delectable fiancé, by any chance?"

Jack seemed suitably embarrassed by her question. "Sorry, slip of the tongue."

"I'll let you off this time. What about May Childs, Joanna? Anything show up there? I know the lady is sadly now dead, but does she have any living relatives we can possibly call and see?"

"I'm still checking on that side of things, boss. I should have something for you later on today. All my focus so far has been on tracing the Ryland family."

"No problem. I expect too much of you at times. What about the Ryland family? What else do we know about them?"

"It would appear that Jeff was one of four boys. Warren, Shaun and Thomas are still alive today, and all live relatively close to their mother."

"Is there a father on the scene?"

"Yes, sorry for omitting to tell you that. William Ryland is in his seventies, still married to Janet and living at the same address. I've written it down for you." Joanna passed Sally a slip of paper with the couple's Suffolk address written on it.

"Excellent news. I'll just ring 'my old man' and see if he can add anything before we set off."

Jack cringed before he grinned at her. "Sounds like a good idea."

Sally walked back into her office, and it was then that she noticed her mobile was still on silent from when she'd entered the prison. Punching in her password, she found a dozen missed messages. She listened to them one by one. They were all from Simon. With each message, his tone became more and more anxious. "Shit. Why didn't I check sooner?" She dialled his number using the landline. "Hey, it's me."

"Oh my, thank God! Where are you?"

"Sorry. I'm back at the station. I've only just realised my phone was on silent and I missed all your messages. Simon, there was no need for you to be quite so worried."

"I'm sorry. It shows I care if nothing else. How did your visit go?"

"I'll put it this way…it was an experience. I'll tell you all about it later, if that's all right?"

"Okay. I suppose the main thing is that you're out of there and back in familiar territory."

"I am. The reason I'm calling, apart from to put your mind at ease, is to see if you're any further forward to identifying the victim?"

"Your girl—Joanna, is it? She sent me over the boy's photo. I've asked the anthropology pathologist to get started on the skull. He's doing it as a favour to me, and he should have something for me in a few days. My expert opinion in the meantime remains the same. We're dealing with a victim between the ages of eleven and thirteen.

Therefore, in all probability, it could be Jeff Ryland. There again, it might not."

"Okay. We've managed to track down his parents, and Jack and I are going over there now."

"Crikey, you can't tell them just yet, Sal."

"Grant me with more sense than that, Simon. They have a right to know that a body has been found in the house next door to where they lived."

"I suppose you're right. Sorry for doubting your way of thinking."

"It's fine. We had the same doubts ourselves as a team. I need to visit them before the reporters get wind of what's going on and start camping on their doorstep, making a nuisance of themselves."

"I'm with you and wholeheartedly agree with the choice you have made."

She laughed. "Thanks for reinforcing that I'm right about this. Look, I have to go, and, Simon…"

"Yes, Sally?"

"Don't worry about me ever doing my day-to-day job, not around here. Nothing truly bad happens in Norfolk compared to the rest of the country."

"Really? I'll bear that in mind in the future when I'm cutting up the victims who come through here. Jeff Ryland being a prime example."

"Ouch! Smart-arse. Maybe I should have said that a little clearer. What I meant to say is that the police in this area have it easier than, say, someone working in London, such as my mate, Lorne. That reminds me, I must touch base with her soon."

"Maybe you could invite her and Tony to the wedding."

"Hey, she's going to be at the top of my list anyway. No fears about that."

"Good. I like them both."

Sally chuckled. "Glad you approve of my friends. It always helps to keep a relationship on the right track."

"I better go before I put my foot in it any more. Glad you're safe. I'll cook us a nice meal tonight."

"What? To celebrate me being safe?"

Simon tutted and hung up.

When Sally walked back into the incident room, DCI Green was scrutinising what was written on the whiteboard. Sally looked over at Jack and rolled her eyes. Forcing a smile on her face, she approached her senior officer and asked, "Hello, sir, to what do we owe the pleasure?"

"Hello, Inspector. I dropped by your office and heard you were in conversation with someone so decided to wait out here for you until you'd finished. Is this the new case?"

"One of them. We've decided to work one of the old cold cases sitting in my office at the same time."

He turned to face her and raised an eyebrow. "Won't that be stretching your team a little?"

"They're a skilled bunch, sir. We can always defer the investigation on one case if things get a little hectic on the other. You know me— I'm not one to let the grass grow under my feet."

"Indeed. If that's how you want to pursue things, who am I to question you at this stage?"

"Thank you, sir. The team are capable of going over two cases at the same time. We've done it in the past with great success."

"At the end of the day, Inspector, you're all judged on your successes—and your failures, too, I might add. We all are."

"I'm fully aware of that, sir, and always have that at the back of my mind during every investigation," Sally said, feeling a tad guilty for the white lie she had just told him.

DCI Green grunted and walked towards the door. "Keep me updated on both cases as you progress, Inspector. Carry on, team."

Sally waited until he had left the room before she saluted him and shook her head. The team were wise enough to remain quiet.

"Are you ready, Jack? We should make a move. We'll grab some lunch on the way."

"Aww... I was hoping we could grab some fish and chips along the seafront once we got there. I know a nice place in that area. Donna and I used to frequent the beach often in our younger days."

"I'll stick with a sandwich, thanks. I wouldn't be able to move this afternoon if I scoffed fish and chips at lunchtime."

"Spoilsport," he mumbled, collecting his jacket from the back of his chair.

"Everyone know what they're doing? Any questions before we go?"

The room fell silent and the three remaining team members got on with their work. Not for the first time, Sally appreciated what a fabulous team she had around her. Everyone was always on the same page and eager to find a solution together. She couldn't remember the last time any of them had fallen out, if ever. She was proud to have them all serving under her, even Jack, who had a slight rebellious streak running through him, which usually reared its head when they were in the car alone. He was a typical ex-serviceman now and again when the orders were flying around. Nine times out of ten, he was a great partner she would hate to lose.

They stopped off at the baker's in the next town, and Sally ate her sandwich while she drove on the open road while Jack ate his in relative comfort. Around an hour and a quarter later, Sally drew the car to a halt outside a small terraced house on a clean, quiet estate.

She took a deep breath before exiting the car. "Let's do this. Leave the talking to me."

"Don't I always?" Jack replied, standing behind her at the front door to the house.

Sally tutted and rang the doorbell.

Within minutes, a woman wearing an apron opened the door. Frowning, she asked, "Hello, can I help?"

Sally extracted her warrant card and flipped it open for the woman to see. "Hello, Mrs. Ryland. I'm DI Sally Parker, and this is my partner, DS Jack Blackman."

Her hand shook as she placed it against her cheek. "No! You're not here to tell me...after all these years... Is he alive?"

CHAPTER 6

BEFORE SALLY HAD a chance to answer, the woman's legs gave way beneath her and she passed out. Both she and Jack rushed at her, but neither of them was quick enough to prevent her from hitting her head against the wall during the fall. Blood trickled from the graze almost immediately.

"Damn. Help me get her inside, Jack. Hello, is there anybody at home?" Sally called out.

There was no response.

Together, they managed to lift the slim woman and took her into the first room they came to, which happened to be the lounge. Jack placed her on the sofa while Sally ran into the kitchen and searched the cupboards for a glass.

"What the hell is going on here? Who are you? And what are you doing in my bloody house?"

Sally almost dropped the glass she was holding, startled by the sound of the man's voice behind her. She withdrew her warrant card from her pocket again. "I'm sorry. I'm a police officer, sir. Are you Mr. Ryland?"

"Yes. Police officer? Who? What are you doing?"

"DI Sally Parker of the Norfolk Constabulary, sir. I'm sorry for the intrusion. Your wife has passed out. I was fetching her a glass of water."

"Janet? Where is she? Is she all right?"

"My partner is sitting with her. She's in the lounge."

"What did you say to her to make her pass out? Have you found him?"

"Sorry, I only introduced myself. Not sure I did anything wrong other than that."

He ran a hand through his light-grey hair and leaned against the worktop. "It's been a living hell all these years, not knowing whether Jeff was dead or alive. I know we have three other sons, and caring for them was tough at times, but we dug deep and got through it. Of course, all this has been worse for Janet to take. It's always worse on the mothers, right?"

"Sometimes it is, sir. Although every member of the family suffers at the same time. Some cope better than others."

"My wife has never worked. She always said it was her job to be at home, looking after the boys, caring for their needs. That's why it hit her like a speeding train. Knocked the stuffing out of her for years. It was almost a decade before she was anywhere near like her old self. She's always been convinced that she failed Jeff. I've told her countless times over the years not to think that way, but it's impossible for her not to. Back then, like it is today, I suppose, it was hard keeping an eye on your kids twenty-four-seven." He shook his head then uttered, "You didn't answer my question. Have you found him?"

A lump formed in Sally's throat when hope rose in the man's eyes. "Why don't we see how your wife is first before I explain?"

"I have a confession to make," he whispered.

Sally's ears immediately pricked up. "Go on, sir," she said, her pulse racing.

"I have the onset of dementia. I'm not sure I'm going to be much support to my wife if I get too upset in there. Is it possible for one of my sons to be here?"

Sally smiled at the man, her sympathy for his condition mixed with the relief that he wasn't about to confess to his son's murder. "Of course. Do you want me to call him?"

"No. I can just about manage that, Inspector. I'm sorry if it's an inconvenience."

"It's not. Please don't think that way. I'll leave you to it and take this in to your wife." She held up the glass of water and left the room. From the hallway, she heard him talking on the phone.

Jack was leaning against the wooden mantelpiece in the lounge. "Everything all right? Only you've been a while."

Sally pushed the door to behind her. "He was trying to get me to tell him what I know, then he dealt a hammer blow."

Jack's eyes widened, then he lowered his voice and asked, "He hasn't admitted to doing it, has he?"

"That was my first thought, too. He explained that he has dementia, and he wanted to make me aware because he's not sure if he's going to be all right to care for his wife well enough during our visit. He's calling one of his sons now to come over and be with them."

"Phew, that's a relief. Oops…that sounded insensitive to his condition. I'm glad he didn't confess to anything, for her sake," Jack said, motioning towards Mrs. Ryland.

"My sentiments exactly."

The lounge door squeaked a little as it opened. William Ryland entered the room, his gaze immediately drawn to his unconscious wife lying on the sofa.

"Everything all right, Mr. Ryland?"

"Yes, Thomas will be here in a few minutes. He works down the high street."

"That's great news. What does Thomas do for a living, sir?"

"He's a bank manager. It's only a small branch, but he has a lot of responsibility, all the same. Sometimes he has to deal with more than a manager does running one of the huge branches in the main cities."

"I can imagine. Is Thomas your eldest son?" Sally asked the question more to see if the man's memory was up to remembering the more important things in life. Though aware there were different stages to the disease, she was unsure how dementia affected people. Fortunately, she had never had to deal with it first-hand.

"Yes, he's the oldest. Don't expect me to remember what age he is, though, and that has nothing to do with my illness. I've always had trouble remembering the ages right from when they were born. Jeff was the youngest, the baby of the family, which is why it probably hit my wife so hard." He crossed the room and smoothed his hand over her head. "Come on, love, wake up. This isn't like you. I need you to be by my side, you know that." He turned to face Sally and Jack. "I'm lost without her. She's such an understanding, sweet soul. We've been through hell since the lad went missing."

"I can imagine. I'm sure she'll come round in a moment or two, sir. What about your other sons? Are they local, too?"

"Yes, we're all relatively close still. After all that's happened, I think it brought us closer together."

"And what do they do for a living?"

"Shaun, the middle lad, he's an accountant, and Warren is a mechanic. He wasn't very academic at school. He used to be, right up until the time Jeff went missing. His disappearance hit the lad hard. I'd say he's not recovered even today. Whereas Shaun and Thomas have got on with their lives. They're both married and have children of their own now. Of course, they watch those kids like a hawk. Refusing to let them out of their sight after what happened with their brother."

Sally smiled. "I think I'd feel the same way if I were in their shoes."

"Dad! Where are you?" a voice sounded from the kitchen.

"In here, Thomas. In the lounge, son."

A tall, slim man in his fifties who was a younger version of his father appeared in the doorway. His gaze drifted around the room and finally ended up on his mother. He rushed over to the sofa and knelt on the floor beside his father. "What happened?"

"She passed out, son. She'll come round in a moment or two."

"Why did she pass out?" he asked, his tone accusatory when he turned to face Sally and Jack.

"Hi, I'm DI Sally Parker, and this is my partner, DS Jack Blackman.

I promise you we didn't get any further than introducing ourselves before your mother passed out."

"I see. She's had an awful lot of heartache to contend with over the years."

"I can imagine."

His mother groaned a little as she started to come around.

"Oh, thank heavens. Welcome back, darling. How are you feeling?" her husband asked, offering his wife the glass of water.

She tried to accept the glass, but her coordination was off, and she missed it. Thomas helped to lift her head and took the glass from his father.

After sipping the water, Mrs. Ryland said, "Oh my, I'm not sure what came over me. My head hurts."

"Hello, Mrs. Ryland. Do you remember us arriving?" Sally walked towards the woman, keeping a little distance behind her son, not wishing to overcrowd anyone.

The woman frowned deeply. "Yes, it's all coming back now. Help me to sit up, will you, Thomas?"

Her son placed the glass on the nearby table and helped his mother to sit up. Her feet slipped to the floor, and she stretched her neck. "Why are you here? Does this have anything to do with my son, Jeff?"

"If I can give you a little background information on who we are, it might help. We've recently set up a cold case team in Norfolk."

"So you're going over old ground? Is that it?" Thomas asked, rising to his feet once he'd settled his mother into position.

"Not really. The case came to my attention, and I know how dreadful it is for families to suffer when there are so many loose ends. I just wanted to reach out to you if only to inform you that you're on our radar, and if something should present itself, then we will be only too happy to reinvestigate your son's case." She could feel Jack's gaze on the back of her head. She was aware she was speaking gobbledegook. She just hoped the family didn't pick up on that.

"None of this makes any sense," Thomas said.

"I'm sorry. It is what it is. Would you mind telling me if your son has made contact with you over the years in any way? Perhaps you've received a phone call where someone was on the other end and didn't speak?"

"Nothing at all, Inspector," Thomas replied, speaking on behalf of his parents.

"I see." Sally felt like she was treading water. "When your brother went missing all those years ago, were there any calls from anyone? Maybe someone who had abducted him, asking for a ransom of sorts?"

"Nothing at all. Jeff simply disappeared while out playing one day," Thomas explained. He walked away from his parents and sat on the edge of the nearest easy chair. He ran a hand through his short grey hair. "We all used to play outside in those days. Never thought of the danger we were putting ourselves into back then. He went out one day and never returned. We set up several search parties in the neighbourhood but without success. This went on for months."

"It must have been dreadful, not knowing."

He nodded. "It was. It's the not knowing that torments your waking days. Mum has been living in shock for years. I'm not surprised she passed out when you turned up. I think the Norfolk police gave up on us decades ago."

"I'm sorry you feel that way. Maybe we can put things right, if you'll let us?"

"Let you? You want to start raking through the dirt again? Put my mother and father through hell? Give them false hopes to latch on to? Don't you think that would be a form of torture for them?"

"I know things will probably be tough to begin with. Maybe you and your brothers would be willing to help us with our enquiries rather than cause any further upset to your parents."

"We're all still upset about this, Inspector. Not just Mum and Dad, although it is ten times worse for them obviously."

"I appreciate that. I truly do. Just give me a few weeks to find the answers."

Thomas glanced over at his parents. The colour had drained not only from his mother's face but also from his father's as well. "You can see my parents' reaction to your visit, Inspector. I'm not sure either of them could go through a lot of useless questions that lead to nowhere."

"Just a few questions, and then we'll leave you alone. How's that?" Sally persisted. It was getting harder not to mention the real reason they were there.

The three of them conferred then reluctantly agreed.

"Go on. Only a few questions, though. Make them count, Inspector," Thomas said reluctantly.

"Thank you. I will. If you can cast your mind back to the time Jeff disappeared, can you tell me anything about your neighbours that didn't sit right with you at the time?"

Thomas looked at his parents. They both seemed perplexed and deep in thought. His father was the first to answer.

He bashed his head with the palm of his hand. "Damn mind. I can't think properly."

"Don't get yourself worked up about this, Dad. Take a breath and let it go for now. What about you, Mum?"

Janet Ryland shook her head. "I can't say I remember anything that was suspicious back then. Wouldn't the police have questioned the neighbours?"

"Probably. What about you, Thomas? Did you hear any gossip at school, perhaps?"

He fell silent, thinking, and then sighed heavily. "Nothing that is coming to mind. We had a few rowdy neighbours playing loud music and a couple of gangs that started up, but nothing major as far as I can remember. Are you referring to anything in particular?"

Sally swallowed. "What about the name May Childs?" She could feel the intensity of Jack's gaze on her back.

"Well, that's a name I haven't heard in years. Do you remember May, William?" Janet asked her husband.

His brow furrowed. "The name rings a bell. I can't for the life of me remember where I know it from."

"She was our next-door neighbour, wasn't she, Mum? A petite lady, if I recall."

"She was indeed, lad. We always used to get on well. Why do you mention her name, Inspector?"

Sally clasped her hands together in front of her and twisted her engagement ring. She decided if she didn't confide in the family now, then she would lose their trust.

"Why the hesitation? What are you so reluctant to tell us?" Thomas asked, rising to his feet and taking a few steps towards the sofa to be near his mother.

"Maybe you remember her erecting a shed in her back garden?" Sally asked rather clumsily.

Janet nodded slowly. "I do, as it happens. It took her years to save up for it. She paid a local man up the road to lay the concrete base and erect it for her. We could see the top of it over our fence."

"That's right, love. It annoyed the hell out of me for weeks—no, *months*—until I put a climbing rose against the fence."

Janet placed a loving hand on her husband's cheek. "How could you forget that, right, love? It became our rose. Every time I was feeling down about Jeff, William used to cut a single rose from the climber and place it in a vase on the table for me. He's such a romantic at heart."

"That's nice. Do you recall the builder's name?"

"It was Bill Drake. He died a few years later, I believe," Janet said.

"That's a shame. Did you know that May died a while back too?"

Janet gasped. "No, I had no idea. How? Natural causes? Because she wasn't that old really."

"Yes, the lady living at your old house found her lying in her bed in two thousand and three." For some reason, Sally connected her gaze with Thomas's.

His eyes narrowed as he stared at her, and she felt uncomfortable.

"How dreadful. She was such a kind lady to us at the time Jeff went missing. Couldn't do enough for us really. She used to help me out weekly with a spot of housework because she could see I wasn't coping very well. Not sure how I would have managed if she hadn't been on hand. You can imagine what it was like living in a household full of men, can't you?"

Sally smiled. "I can. I fear men are no different today as they were back then, Mrs. Ryland."

Thomas paced the floor. Sally feared what was about to take place next.

"Enough! Enough of this. Why? Why come here and ask about the neighbours? What's going on, Inspector? I'm warning you—if you don't give me an adequate answer, then I will take it up with your superior. Tell us!"

Sally puffed out her cheeks and took a step backwards, towards her partner, drawing the energy she needed to carry on. "Right, okay, I feel as though you've pushed me into a corner here. I have some news, but I need you to listen to me very carefully and not jump to any conclusions just yet."

"Get on with it, for God's sake," Thomas insisted, the skin around his eyes developing a sudden angry twitch.

Sally faced Jack. When he shrugged, she turned back to the Rylands. "We received a call from the new owners of May Child's old house yesterday morning. They had decided to pull down the shed and smashed up the old concrete base, only to find...bones."

"What?" Thomas asked, incredulity spreading across his stern face.

"What does she mean, Thomas?" Janet asked, gripping her husband's hand tightly.

"I'm waiting to hear the punchline myself, Mum. Go on, Inspector. What are you telling us without uttering the actual words?"

"The pathologist and his team went to the premises, and after careful digging, they revealed the remains of a body. At this point, we have not yet identified that body."

Janet screamed, scaring everyone in the room. Her husband got to his feet and pummelled his head against the wall until Thomas intervened. He hugged his father to his chest.

Sally rushed over to the sofa to comfort Janet. She placed a hand over the woman's. "Please, we have to be cautious not to think the obvious. The only reason we have come here today is to tell you in person that the remains had been found rather than you hear it in a news bulletin. We don't know that they belong to your son."

"When will you know?" Thomas asked.

"It could be days, or it could take weeks to complete a reconstruction of the skull. Please, you have to bear with us on this."

"Surely you know more than you're letting on. Isn't it obvious that this is Jeff?"

"The last thing we want to do is jump to any conclusions without any evidence to back up such claims." She sighed and squeezed the sobbing woman's hand. "All I can tell you is the pathologist is pretty certain the bones belong to a child between the ages of eleven and thirteen."

Janet withdrew her hand from Sally's and covered her face as the wailing struck up again. "Jeff...it's my Jeff. I know it is," she cried out in between the sobs.

Thomas guided his father to the chair and crouched on the floor in between his parents. "Mum, Dad, hear me out. We have to listen to what the inspector says and take this news with a pinch of salt until they've formally identified the body. There's no point in you both upsetting yourselves like this."

Janet shook her head in disbelief. "No point! How can you say that, Thomas? You don't know what it's been like all these years. To lie awake at night, envisioning all sorts happening to my child. I know this is him. It *has* to be him. After all these years of not knowing where he was, and all the time, he was a mere few feet away from us. I should have known that. In my heart, I should have known he was within spitting distance of us. Why did we move from there? He was there all that time, and we deserted him..." Fresh tears emerged, and her voice trailed off.

"You mustn't think like that, Mrs. Ryland. It would be best not to go down that route for your own sanity. Let's wait to get the formal identification before we begin any self-recriminations," Sally said, her own eyes misting up, reflecting the woman's obvious pain.

Janet wiped the tears away and sat upright. "Thinking back, I believe the shed went up a few days after Jeff went missing. I seem to remember thinking how inconsiderate it was of May to carry out the work during the torturous time for us. When it was all over, she came round and apologised for the disturbance. She told me that the builder had a huge renovation job coming up and if he didn't erect the shed then it would be months before he would be able to get back to complete the job, if the winter weather permitted him to do it."

"That's really helpful, Janet. It'll put a timeline on things once the identification process is complete."

Janet's eyes glazed over. She started to speak then stopped herself. When she finally had the courage to say what was on her mind, everyone in the room stiffened a little. "You don't suppose May had anything to do with his…disappearance, do you?"

Sally exhaled a large breath. "It really is too soon to tell that. There are a lot of avenues for us to explore before we come to any conclusions."

Thomas grunted. "It was either May or that builder she employed. A lot of good knowing that is going to do us—they're both dead now!"

"That's the problem we have dealing with cold cases. Quite often, the witnesses or the person guilty of committing the crime have died in the interim."

Thomas's arms flew out to the side and lowered again to slap his thighs. "That's marvellous news. Just what we wanted to hear, Inspector."

Sally shrugged. "I'm sorry. I thought we were being open with each other. I deal in facts, Mr. Ryland. Sometimes when these facts surface, the news isn't always what people want to hear. Rest assured, my team and I will endeavour to probe into every aspect of the case to obtain the information we need for a conviction, if that is at all possible. If the culprit or culprits have died in the interim, then there is very little anyone can do about it." She chewed the inside of her cheek, ashamed she had allowed Thomas to wind her up.

Thomas stared at her, scowling. Sally suddenly felt self-conscious and uncomfortable under his gaze.

Thankfully, Jack chose that instant to speak. "I think we should leave you now."

Sally swivelled to look at him and winked. "I agree. I'll leave you

my card, along with my promise that I will keep chasing the pathologist for the results several times a day until they come through."

"I think that's a wise decision on your part, Inspector, to leave us
now you've stirred up all this emotional turmoil without any actual
evidence."

"I'm sorry you feel that way, Mr. Ryland. I was merely putting
myself in your mother's shoes. I would want to know if there was an
inkling my son's remains had been found."

"Leave it, Thomas. The inspector is right—she was damned if she
told us and damned if she didn't. Life deals us many blows during
our existence, some lower than others. I'm glad the inspector and her
partner have shared what they know. Maybe now the healing
process can begin at last. If it turns out to be Jeff. I'll do my best to
keep my emotions in check as much as I can until he's been
identified."

"Thank you for understanding, Janet. One last thing before I go. I
don't suppose you have any possessions of Jeff's lying around, have
you? Such as a comb, perhaps, or some of his baby teeth for DNA
purposes. Something we'll be able to match to if the pathologist
requires it."

Janet nodded and held out a hand for Thomas to assist her to
stand. "I'll see what I can find. There are a couple of boxes of Jeff's
things in the spare room. I got rid of a lot of things during the course
of the move but not everything. Well, just in case he came back."

When Janet left the room, an awkwardness shrouded Sally. She
avoided eye contact with Thomas, hoping that would prevent any
further conflict between them.

"I don't understand," William muttered, shaking his head slightly.

Thomas sat on the chair beside his father and flung an arm around
his shoulders. "What don't you understand, Dad?"

"Is Jeff coming home to us or not?"

Thomas glanced up, and his eyes narrowed as if accusing Sally of
putting his father through unnecessary anguish. "Not yet, Dad. Hopefully one day."

"Ah, that's good then. It'll be nice to have the lad home after all these years. I wonder where he's been up until now. Strange he hasn't been to see us. You boys used to be so close when you were younger."

"Yes, Dad. Let's not dwell on things like that for now."

Luckily, with the air in the room getting colder by the second, Janet returned and offered Sally a comb she had found, plus a small jar which held several of Jeff's teeth. "Have you got a plastic bag on you, Jack?"

He withdrew one from his pocket.

"Is that all you need now?" Thomas asked impatiently.

Sally opened the bag, and Janet dropped the comb and jar inside. After securing the bag, Sally nodded. "That's all for now. Thank you for your cooperation. Hopefully, I'll be in touch again soon with the information you need."

"I'll show you out," Thomas announced, marching towards the door.

"Thank you, dear. I'm sorry we were all so wrapped up in our grief to really appreciate what a difficult job this must have been for you to deal with."

Sally held out her hand for Janet to shake, and the woman clenched it in both her hands and smiled. "Don't worry. I won't let you down, Janet."

"I'm sure about that, my dear. Thank you."

When Sally and Jack left the room, Sally could hear a confused William ask his wife who the strangers were in his house. Sally felt sorry for what the family continued to have to deal with.

Thomas was at the front door, holding it open for them, his expression blank. "We'll see you again soon. No doubt when you have the evidence to back up your claims," he said sharply.

"I'm sorry if I've upset you, Mr. Ryland. I've explained already why I felt the need to come and visit your parents. There really is no need for you to be angry over this issue."

"I'm sorry my overprotectiveness towards my parents is coming across as me being angry, Inspector. I guess we all have our crosses to bear in this life."

"We do, indeed. My partner and I will visit your parents once the

ID has been made. We'll also need to interview the whole family when we return, too. Will you ensure your brothers understand that we'll be contacting them?"

"I will. Although I'm not really sure we'll be able to tell you anything that will help you solve the case, if it turns out to be Jeff."

"Any information we can pick up will help, even if this happened decades ago." Sally walked past him, and Jack followed. "We'll be in touch soon. Sorry to drag you away from your work."

"It was my choice. Goodbye, Inspector." He closed the door.

They were settled back in the car before either of them spoke.

"Well, that went well," Jack said.

"You think I was wrong telling them, don't you? Go on, be honest, Jack. I have broad shoulders, in case you haven't noticed."

"Don't get antsy with me. I said right from the word go that I thought it would be wrong telling them."

"What else was I supposed to do? Thomas twigged virtually straight away once I started asking questions about the neighbours."

"Yeah!"

"What's that tone supposed to mean?" she asked, turning the key in the ignition and pulling away from the house.

"Why was he so shitty? His attitude stank to me."

"He apologised for being overprotective. I'm willing to put his manner down to that."

"You're too fond of thinking the best of people. I'm on the line with him."

Sally stopped the car at a red light and faced him. "Are you saying you think he had something to do with his brother's disappearance, or death, if that's what comes to light?"

Jack kept his attention focussed on the road ahead and shrugged. "I'm just saying his attitude sucked back there, as if he was shielding something from us." He pointed at the road.

The lights had changed, and she pressed her foot on the accelerator. "I think you're reading too much into it, matey. He was abrupt, granted. How do you think you would react if two coppers turned up on your doorstep thirty-odd years later, like we did?"

"Okay, you've got me there. All I'm saying is we shouldn't discount him from our enquiries."

"Noted. But for the record, I think you're pissing in the wind on this one."

Jack shook his head in despair. "Whatever. Want me to check through the other neighbours in the area at that time when we get back?"

"Yep, either this afternoon or first thing tomorrow. I want to work on the other case with Jordan over the next few days, at least until Simon formerly identifies the remains."

"I think you have the easier job," he grumbled.

"You're so wrong there. If you had dealings with this Christopher Abbott, you'd be begging me to get involved in the Ryland case."

"I guess we'll never know."

The rest of the journey was spent in virtual silence as a mixture of emotions ran through Sally. On the one hand, she hoped the remains would turn out to be Jeff Ryland's, enabling the rest of the family to get on with their lives finally. On the other, she hoped it wouldn't be him because she feared what knowing the truth would do to both William and Janet. She imagined the guilt they were probably feeling could intensify tenfold.

They arrived back at the station around four thirty, and by the time they had divulged to the rest of the team what they had learnt from the Rylands, Sally was exhausted, both mentally and physically. "All right, guys, I don't know about you, but I'm done in and ready for home. I feel drained. Let's call it a day and begin afresh in the morn-ing. Jordan, how has your research gone today on the Hathaway case?"

"Fair to middling, boss. Want me to go through the details with you now or in the morning?"

"In the morning. My brain is frazzled beyond comprehension right now."

She dismissed the team and collected her handbag and coat from the office then jumped back into her car to venture home. She'd only travelled a few streets when she had the strangest feeling that someone was following her.

Don't be an idiot, there's no one there, looking in her rear-view mirror. She really was tired if she was imagining such a thing.

Simon greeted her at the front door when she arrived home. He gathered her in his arms immediately, sensing that she needed a cuddle. He smoothed a hand over her head and lovingly kissed her forehead. "Have you had a tough day, baby?"

Tilting her head, she glanced up at him. "How could you tell? I'll be fine after a few glasses of wine."

They shared a kiss, then Simon released her and led her through to the kitchen. He stopped at the cupboard under the stairs, opened the small door and took out a bottle of vintage red wine he'd been saving from one of the racks. In the kitchen, he gestured for her to have a seat at the table and poured them both a glass of the fruity wine.

Sally sipped from her glass and savoured the fabulous taste before she swallowed. "Wow, that's really rather special. What year is it?"

"It's a two thousand and seven. A special Californian wine I've been saving. I heard the price was about to skyrocket and bought a case of it."

Sally turned the bottle around to read the label. "Saxum James Berry red. I have to admit I've never heard of half the wines you have in your collection."

"Good. I love sharing something new with you each day."

Sally smiled, all the tension of the day evaporating, the way it always did when they were together. "What's on the menu tonight?"

"I have a couple of steaks in the fridge if you fancy one?"

"Steak and chips?"

"Why not? Let's enjoy a glass of wine first, and you can help me prepare the dinner, if you're up to it. You look exhausted, love."

"Sounds like an exceptional plan to me, and yes, I'm up for it. This will go a long way towards putting things right, though, I hope. How was your day? Any point in me asking how the Ryland case is going? Damn, I almost forgot. I have something for you." She left the table and went back into the hallway to retrieve her bag. She extracted the plastic bag, which she had asked Jack to pop inside a proper evidence bag along with the necessary paperwork and placed it on the table in front of Simon.

"What's this? I know it's a comb and some teeth, but why are you giving it to me?"

"It's a long shot. I asked the Rylands to supply something that would likely have Jeff's DNA on, in case you needed it in the future."

"Good thinking. You're not just a pretty face after all."

Heat rose in her cheeks. "Hope it helps. The mother and father are still beside themselves after all these years. Mrs. Ryland actually passed out when she first laid eyes on us."

"Oh no. Was she all right?"

"Yes. I wasn't going to tell them about the remains, but when I started asking questions about the neighbours, the son sort of twigged where I was leading and forced me into a corner. The father has early signs of dementia. I hope the news doesn't worsen his condition when we eventually reveal the truth."

"Maybe it was wrong to visit them until we're a hundred percent sure."

Sally shrugged. "I had to. You know what the media are like. Once they get wind of something like this, it'll be out there in a flash. I'm sure the family would have been forming a lynch mob if I hadn't gone to see them, yes?"

"You're probably right. It's a tough call to make for you. Sorry for adding to your stress."

She reached across the table and placed a hand over his. "You haven't. You couldn't add to my stress even if you tried."

"What about the other case you're working on? You've travelled a fair few miles today, haven't you?"

"You're not wrong." She shuddered as the memory of visiting Abbott in Norwich entered her mind. "He's such a slimy bastard. He was testing me all the time I was with him."

"Sounds horrendous. Will you have to return to the prison to see him again?"

Sally turned her glass by the stem, and his hand tightened over her other hand.

"Sal? What is it?"

"He wants me to go back with the crime scene photos of the three girls he murdered."

"That's gross. Why?"

"I've heard of it before. I'm sure there's a name for the condition somewhere in the psychologist's handbook. Some prisoners choose to do it, so they can relive the crimes and the sensations they felt when they committed their heinous acts."

"You can't bow to that kind of pressure, surely?"

Sally dropped her gaze to the table and shrugged. "He has me over a barrel."

"How? Sally, look at me."

She glanced up. Concern swam in his eyes. "One of his victims —at least we think she is—the girl's mother is terminally ill with cancer. She needs to know where her daughter's body is so that she can hold the girl's funeral before she dies."

He threw himself back against his chair. "Oh crap, that's awful. I still don't get why he has you over a barrel, though, love."

"If I supply him with the crime scene photos, then he's going to tell me where he buried the girl's body, and possibly the other girls he was suspected of killing at the time he was sentenced."

"I see. Wow, I don't know what to suggest in that case."

"Not only that, but talking to him today, I managed to glean from him that there are probably more victims out there. The original case suspected that he was guilty of possibly killing six girls. However, by what he said today, I believe that there may be another four girls he likely abducted. Who's to say whether he killed them or not?"

"Jesus! He sounds a twisted individual. I'm worried about you going back to prison to see him. Can't you pass the baton over to Jack? I'd feel happier if you did."

Sally tutted. "Hey, we've broken a golden rule tonight by discussing our workload. I'm starving. Let's crack on with dinner, yes?"

"You're impossible to deal with at times, Sally Parker."

She smiled and winked at him. "I know. That's why you love me."

CHAPTER 7

THE REST of the team were all seated at their desks when Sally arrived at work the following morning. "Wow, you guys really do make an inspector proud, without even realising it."

Each of them looked at her, wearing a puzzled expression.

"Oh, right, you mean by showing up for work before you," Jack said as the penny dropped.

"Doh! Yes. Let me grab a coffee and check through the dreaded post, and I'll be with you in a tick." Waiting in her sun-filled office was a pile of letters, which she swiftly opened and sorted into piles of importance, promising to deal with them during the course of the day. After finishing her coffee, she rejoined the rest of the team in the incident room.

"Okay, let's discuss where we are. Joanna, any news on tracking down the neighbours from back in eighty-five?"

"I've found a few, boss. Not many, but enough to be going on with, I reckon."

"It's a long shot, but how many of those are still living in this area?"

"Three of the five I'm searching for, so far."

Sally nodded. "That's better than nothing. Try and find the others today, and Jack and I will make arrangements to visit them tomorrow."

"Don't forget we've got the family to interview, as well," Jack reminded her, scratching the side of his head.

"I hadn't. What are you trying to say, Jack?"

He shrugged. "Nothing. I'll keep my mouth shut."

Sally laughed. "There's no need for you to do that. Let's get things organised first, and then, if I find we're snowed under with people to visit, I'll divide the workload up. How's that?"

"Sounds like a mighty fine plan to me, boss. I'd hate for us to get overwhelmed."

"Quite right. Once the research element has been carried out, if it turns out there are dozens of people to interview, we'll all get involved in that side of things. I'd already thought about that, Jack, so don't worry. It's not as if we need to keep a member of staff here all the time, manning the phone like in the good old days, is it?"

"Fair point."

"Good. Now that's sorted. Anything else we need to highlight on the Ryland case before I move on?"

The team all shook their heads. Sally had arranged with the desk sergeant for the delivery of another whiteboard to the incident room. She stepped towards the clean one and picked up the black marker pen. "Okay, if the rest of you want to crack on with the Ryland case, Jordan and I will start on the Hathaway case. Just ignore us."

Jack grumbled. "Will it be all right if we overhear something and want to chime in now and again?"

"As per usual, you mean, partner? Sure it is." Sally winked at Jordan, who sniggered in response.

"Right, Jordan. I left you researching any possible missing young women or girls around the time of Abbott's arrest. What did you manage to find out?"

Jordan pulled a sheet of paper off his desk and handed it to Sally.

She let out a long whistle. "Bloody hell. You did all this yesterday?"

Jordan nodded. "I might have taken it home with me to finish, but basically, yes. I jotted down most of that during my shift."

"Did anything jump out at you once you'd completed the task?" she asked, scanning the information.

Jordan had placed each of the women's names in circles, along with the date she was reported missing and the day that particular woman's body had been discovered. Only three of the names had the last snippet of information alongside them.

Sighing, Jordan tapped his pen on the desk. "I guess the thing that truly struck me was that all the women ranged from the ages of seventeen up to twenty-one. All except for the little girl, Lynn Jackman."

Sally nodded her understanding as to what he was referring to. "And she was only ten, if I recall correctly."

"Exactly. Why did he change his MO?"

Sally nodded. "It's something I should ask him when I next visit him."

"It would be interesting to find out, boss. Maybe something we can look at for future cases."

"Good thinking. He's going to be a tough one to crack, that's for sure. I'll need to have my wits about me when I visit him again. There's no doubt about that. Maybe I should have a word with the governor. See if Abbott has had any visits from a psychiatrist since he was convicted. Anyway, let's stick to the facts for now." She scribbled the information that Jordan had supplied on the board. "Here we go then. According to your research, Karen Pitts, nineteen, disappeared on March eleventh. Her body was found four days later in a boggy area not far from her home by some walkers."

"Strange that he didn't try to bury the body, boss."

"Mark of his inexperience, perhaps?"

"Maybe. All the signs are telling us that."

Sally wrote down the second name in capital letters. "Sophie Johnson. This is one of the girls from the missing list, right?"

Jordan nodded.

"We're unsure at this point if she has anything to do with this case or not. Judging by the timeline, I'm inclined to think along the same lines as you and say yes. Do me a favour, Jordan, will you print off photos of all the suspected victims for me while I write up the rest of the details? It might be good to see if there's a pattern in the girls' appearance."

"Damn. I knew I had to do something first thing. Sorry, boss. I'm on it now."

"No need to apologise. You've already gone the extra mile on this one."

Jordan tapped his keyboard, and seconds later, the printer sitting next to Joanna churned into action. He jumped out of his chair, collected the sheets of paper and took them back to his desk. With a pair of scissors, he cut around the girls' heads and stood alongside Sally as he stuck them to the board with Blu Tack. Before long, between them, they had filled the board with all the information. Sally stood back and folded her arms. Tilting her head from side to side, she reread the details.

"Let's dispel the doubts and take what you found out about the girls as being fact from now on, okay?"

"I researched it thoroughly, boss. Considered what you said about Abbott's priorities for picking up a girl a few days after he'd disposed of the previous one. I must admit, some of the girls were guesswork only because the previous victim's body hadn't shown up. If that makes sense?"

"Perfect sense to me. Also, how many young girls tend to go missing around the same time? It seems wise to note down the names that showed up on the missing persons list going by the dates. We can always swap the names out in the future, however, I trust your research to be accurate."

"Thanks, boss. That means a lot."

"So, Sophie Johnson is twenty-one. She went missing on March seventeenth but was never found. Which leads us on to Tania Thomason. What do we know about her?" Sally picked up the original file and flicked through it. "Ah, here we are. Again, her body has never been discovered. What we do know is that her handbag was found tucked under the passenger seat of Abbott's car when it was forensically examined."

"At least we can point the finger at him on that one. Did he offer her a ride, perhaps?"

"Possibly. There was nothing in the file to say how he chose his victims. Maybe he trawled the streets, on the lookout for girls in need of a lift and pulled up alongside them to offer his services. Who knows? I'll add it to my list of questions to ask the pervert when I see him next. Right, we have another new victim that you added to the list —Millie Potter, eighteen. Reported missing four days after Tania disappeared."

"Again, we need to put a question mark alongside her name."

Sally did just that. "Then we have Emily Norton, who was seventeen. Again, I recognise the name from the file." She picked up the folder and jotted down the details alongside Emily's name. "More evidence located in Abbott's car. This time, a half-smoked cigarette. Her body has never been found, but she went missing on the twenty-seventh of March. Moving on, we have Michele Denton, aged twenty-one. She was reported missing on the thirtieth of March. Her body was extracted from the River Yare on April tenth. Examining the timelines, that seems a long gap in between, compared to the other girls."

"I suppose it depends on when he dumped her in the river and how long it took for someone to find her," Jordan chipped in.

"Excellent point. Let me try and find the PM documentation." She studied the notes, and according to the pathologist, Michele could have been in the water up to five days before her body was found. "Five days, give or take. Which makes sense timewise. Then we have another girl from your list, Carina Sanders, nineteen, who went missing on April the twelfth. After which, we have poor Katrina Hathaway, eighteen, whose mother is dying of cancer. She disappeared on April seventeenth." Sally sighed heavily before she continued. "The penultimate victim is yet another girl from your list, Jasmine Winkleman, also eighteen, who vanished on April twentieth. Which leads us to Lynn Jackman, whose body was found in Abbott's car when his vehicle was stopped by the police for having bald tyres, thankfully. If that hadn't happened, Lord knows how many more victims we would be searching for today."

"Doesn't bear thinking about, boss. So, where do we go from here?"

"We need to phone each of the families of the girls who are still missing. Just to make sure the girls haven't contacted them since."

"Shall I tell the families that we're reinvestigating the cases?"

"Yes, tell them we're tentatively looking into things at the moment and hope to have some good news for them in the near future."

Jordan chewed the inside of his mouth before he spoke again. "It's bound to raise their hopes, isn't it?"

"Judging by the Rylands' reaction, yes, you're right. Just ensure you tamper that down to begin with, and we should be all right. The last thing we want to do is cause any more unnecessary heartbreak to these people.

"Of course. If you're up to it and if you think the relatives would welcome a face-to-face visit, perhaps go and see them today. Although I'd steer clear of the new names you added to the list until after I've had a chance to gauge Abbott's reaction to them."

"I can do that, if that's the route you want me to take, boss. Do you want me to ask where they think the girls went missing?"

"That would be great, Jordan. It would be excellent if we can build some kind of map as to the area he was using. You never know, it might lead us eventually to where the other girls are buried or at least to the place where he was holding them. According to the file, Forensics went over his house and found no evidence at all that the girls were either held or killed there."

"Leave it with me, boss. I'll keep you informed on how things are progressing."

Sally squeezed his shoulder as she passed his chair. "Good man. Right, Jack, I think we should set off to try and find the Ryland brothers. Why don't we start with Shaun Ryland first?"

"Okay, he's an accountant, I believe. I've got his work address here if you want to visit him there."

"Makes sense to me. Bring all the addresses you've gathered with you. We'll hit all the brothers this morning." She glanced up at the clock. It was already approaching eleven o'clock. "Damn, it's later than I thought. Correct that, this morning and the early part of the afternoon."

CHAPTER 8

THE ACCOUNTANCY FIRM was larger than Sally had anticipated. Shaun Ryland was listed as a partner in the firm. Gesturing at the words etched on the window, she said, "He seems to have done well in the world, just like his other brother, Thomas."

"Yeah, looks that way. Strange that Warren didn't go down the same financial route as his brothers. He opted to become a car mechanic instead."

Sally chuckled. "Maybe there weren't enough brains to go around. Stupid observation. Ignore that."

"Take it as read," Jack grumbled, rolling his eyes to the sky.

Sally grinned and entered the building. A friendly brunette was sitting at a desk, but she stood up and approached the counter separating her from the public. "Hello there. Can I help you?"

Sally held up her warrant card and introduced them. "DI Sally Parker and DS Jack Blackman. We'd like a word with Shaun Ryland if it's possible?"

"Ah, I see. I'm afraid he's in a meeting with a client for the next thirty minutes or so. It's with a huge client of ours, so I can't interrupt him, either. Sorry."

"That's a shame. We'll go and grab something to eat and return in half an hour then. If you can let him know to expect us once he's finished his meeting?"

"Of course. May I ask what it's in connection with? He's bound to ask."

"I'd rather not say. It's a personal matter, for him anyway."

She nodded and returned to her seat. "See you in a while then."

Sally and Jack left the office and turned right to go down the high street. "I spotted a small café when I drove past. I'll shout you some lunch."

"That's generous of you."

"Within reason. Nothing fancy, if they do it."

"As if I would," Jack replied, a large grin stretching his lips to the limit.

The menu was extensive for a small place, though it comprised of mostly sandwiches and paninis. Sally decided on an egg mayonnaise sandwich while Jack opted for a bacon panini. They ordered a couple of large lattes to accompany their lunches.

While they waited for their lunch to arrive, Sally took out her notebook and wrote down some questions she wanted to ask Shaun when they finally got to meet him. "Anything in particular you can think of to ask him, Jack?"

"Not off the top of my head. Let's hope he's not as feisty as Thomas."

"I'm hoping that was a one-off for him. He was probably concerned about his parents' well-being after receiving the devastating news."

"That's just it—we haven't had the news confirmed yet."

"I know. There's still a possibility that it was Jeff we were referring to, though. I can't imagine what that must be like to deal with. Let's hope he's more accepting of us when we show up at the bank to see him later."

A petite waitress appeared and placed their lunch on the table, along with their drinks. "There you go. I hope you enjoy it."

Sally smiled up at the woman. "Thank you, I'm sure we will."

"Er…do you have any ketchup?" Jack asked.

"Of course. I'll be right back." She swept away and, true to her word, came back a few seconds later with a Heinz ketchup bottle.

"Thanks. Can't have a bacon sarnie without ketchup," Jack said, accepting the bottle and squeezing a vast amount on his panini.

The waitress sniggered and returned to the serving hatch to pick up the next order.

"Good God, man, you're so uncouth. How much ketchup? I'll be surprised if you can taste the bacon at that rate."

Jack pulled a face at her. "Good job it's my lunch and not yours then. Enjoy your egg mayo."

Sally placed half a sandwich to her lips. "I will, thanks," she said then took a small bite. The sandwich was filled to capacity, and as she bit into it, the mayonnaise oozed out the side of her mouth. She quickly wiped the excess on a serviette. When she looked up to see if Jack had noticed, a blob of ketchup slipped from his panini and landed on his navy-blue tie as he bit into it.

"Damn and blast. I haven't got a spare tie with me."

She sniggered. "I'm sure it'll clean up. It's dark enough. Take more care with the rest of it. I told you that you'd put too much ketchup on."

"It must get tedious being right all the time, boss."

She shrugged. "Not really."

They finished their lunch without further mishaps, paid the bill and strolled back to the accountancy firm. A well-dressed man walked out of the building and hopped into a shiny Daimler.

"Nice car. Must have cost a packet," Jack noted. His gaze stuck with the car as it smoothly reversed out of the slot and purred away.

"Wouldn't be my choice of car if I had the dosh."

Jack raised an eyebrow at her. "Get you! I'll take what's on offer and be grateful for it."

"Each to their own, eh? If we all liked the same vehicles, a lot of the manufacturers would go out of business. Come on, let's get this over with."

A tall man wearing a pin-stripe suit, with slicked-back black hair that was going grey at the sides, was talking to the receptionist when they walked in.

The receptionist pointed in their direction. "Here they are now, Mr. Ryland."

Sally smiled at the gentleman, who eyed them warily. "You wanted to see me?"

"If you have the time, sir? We met your mother, father and brother yesterday. Perhaps they informed you of our visit."

Shaun Ryland looked sideways at the receptionist then back at Sally. "Ah, yes. Thomas rang me last night. Why don't we go through to my office? My next appointment isn't for another half an hour, but I'd like to squeeze lunch in between, if that's possible?"

"Of course. We shouldn't take up too much of your time, sir."

"Linzi, can you pop and get me a ham and cheese panini when you have a second?"

"Of course. I'll drop the latch on the door now and fetch it for you."

Shaun nodded his appreciation and placed ten pounds on the counter. Then he marched down the hallway, Sally and Jack close on his heels. The office was medium in size, and the large cherrywood desk dominated the room. The rest of the furniture consisted of matching filing cabinets and several bookshelves. Sally could tell immediately what type of clients used the accountancy firm—no Joe Blogs, that was for sure.

"Take a seat. How can I help?"

Sally and Jack sat opposite Shaun. She extracted her notebook. "We just wanted to see if you could remember around the time your brother went missing."

"Of course I can remember. The pain and anguish we all suffered at the time is etched into my mind and haunts my every waking moment. Thomas told me that you think you've discovered Jeff's body."

"I didn't actually say that. It's yet to be confirmed by the pathologist. A body was found at your ex-neighbour's house, buried in the back garden under the shed."

"So Thomas said. Surely, it must be Jeff, right? Unless some other kid went missing around that time. Is that likely, Inspector?"

"I'd rather keep things as they are for now, Mr. Ryland. I'd hate to suggest it was your brother and be proved wrong farther down the line. That could cause untold damage to you and your parents, and I'm just not prepared to do that to you all."

"I can understand you being cautious in that respect. How can I help then?"

"We need to ascertain your brother's final whereabouts or actions. Can you help us with that at all?"

"Not really. I was a few years older than Jeff. You know what it's like—the last thing you want is your younger brother hanging around with you when you're out with your friends. Of course, now that I'm older and have had time to reflect on that line of thinking, I wish I had taken more interest in what Jeff got up to back then. Maybe if I had, he'd still be with us today. There's not a day goes by that guilt doesn't prod a finger at my chest."

"I'm sorry to hear that. Often in cases of child abduction, it comes to light that it's extremely difficult for the family not to have recriminations. Even though there was little that could have been done at the time."

"That's exactly right. None of us could have done anything. Jeff was a likeable lad. He had a lot of friends and was popular. We never got the impression that he needed his big brothers watching out for him. Like I have said already, the guilt is a bitter pill to swallow."

"I can understand that. If you can cast your mind back to around the time he went missing, did you ever notice anything out of the ordinary? Someone hanging around? A stranger, perhaps?"

He placed his forefingers on either side of his head and fell silent for a few seconds. "No, I can't think of anything or anyone that fits the bill. We used to be a close-knit community as far as I can remember. The parents always watched out for all the kids on the street, not just their own. That's why it was such a shock when Jeff went missing because no one ever saw anything that caused them an ounce of suspicion."

"That is strange. Can you remember what your neighbour was like?"

"My neighbour? May Childs, you mean?"

"Yes. The remains of the victim were found in her garden. Someone must have put them there."

"What? And you think May has had something to do with this?"

Sally shrugged. "It's a line of enquiry we need to go down to search for possible answers."

"All I remember about May was that she was small in stature and always kind to the children, in spite of having none of her own. She wasn't married as far as I can recall. Most of the people in our neighbourhood were married. She stood out on that count, but I wouldn't say it made her an outcast in the slightest."

"That's good to know. Did she ever invite kids to the house?"

His face screwed up. "Entice them in with the intention of killing them off? Is that what you're implying?"

"It's something we'd be careless not to consider, given the circumstances."

He shook his head in horror. "I can't recollect ever getting a bad feeling about the woman when I was in her presence. Mum used to be really close to her back then. Surely, if Mum had picked up any bad vibes, she wouldn't have had anything to do with her."

"It's not unheard of for people who abduct children to wear a mask for the general public."

He ran a hand through his hair. "Never. I just can't believe it would be true of her. I'm not saying I've come across people of that ilk before, but bloody hell, never in a million years would I have suggested she'd be involved in something so sordid."

"I'll note it down. We're going to have to canvass the neighbourhood again. I know years have passed, but there might be the odd neighbour living there still."

"I'm sure they'll say the same thing. Have you checked your records to see if there were any paedophiles living in the area at the time?"

"We're doing that now. The trouble is, people who abused children weren't labelled as such back then."

"I see. There must have been some form of records for perverts documented, though, right?"

"Of course. We're searching now but not having much luck, I'm afraid."

"In what respect, Inspector?"

"That nothing is highlighted in that area around the time you lived there. If there were any records of that nature, something would have shown up by now."

"I appreciate how hard a task this is for you to reinvestigate the case after thirty-three years. Please stick with it. Even if the body turns out *not* to be Jeff, it belonged to someone, and of course, Jeff is still missing after all these years."

"Our job is never easy, Mr. Ryland. The more information we can gather, the more likely we are to succeed in finding out what truly happened to Jeff. What are the odds on your brother running away from home?"

He shook his head vehemently. "It just wasn't in him to do that. Jeff loved his family. We were a happy family during our childhood. Mum and Dad rarely had to discipline us at all. We were brought up to recognise right from wrong. Which is why I don't think Jeff would ever run off. Even if he did, he wouldn't have lasted for long. He was totally reliant on what Mum did for him. She cossetted him because he was the baby of the family. She did it in turn with each of us as we were born."

"Usual displays of affections in public and behind closed doors?"

"All the time. She loved us all equally—still does—but she always doted on the youngest child, whoever that was at the time. Jeff had more than his fair share of affection because he remained the youngest. By that I mean that she didn't have any more kids after him."

"That much I gathered. Which is why it probably hit your mother so hard. Was it her idea to move or your father's?"

He shrugged. "I'm not sure. They announced it jointly once the decision had been made to leave. As a family, we never questioned our parents' decisions. Our childhood, after Jeff went missing, dissolved pretty damn quickly, I can tell you. Dad insisted that we all knuckle down to work at school and when we went on to college. People didn't tend to go to university in those days. Warren was the only one who didn't knuckle down. He was the closest in age to Jeff, and I suppose the most sentimental out of all of us. There are days now when he drifts off if you're holding a conversation with him."

"That's a shame. In our experiences, people deal with grief in different ways. He possibly found it tougher, being only a few years older than Jeff."

"He did. He definitely went into his shell, and he's kind of remained there ever since, if you ask me."

"Really? Even after all these years, he's never managed to get past Jeff disappearing like that?"

"Never. He's the only one of us who has never married or had a regular girlfriend he could settle down with. We've always put it down to guilt. Such a sensitive lad. He has a heart of gold, will do anything for you. Thomas and I aren't really handy and don't have a clue about DIY around the house. Warren will drop by and have the problem sorted within hours. He's very handy in that respect, but he gave up on his studies the day Jeff went missing. None of us realised how close he was to Jeff, not until he'd gone. Obviously, we all missed him terribly. It was just that whatever we felt as a family, Warren seemed to take all the grief on himself and failed to shake it off when the rest of us decided not to dwell on matters that were out of our control. If that makes sense?"

"It does. We'll be sure to remember that when we question him. We'll go easy. Don't worry."

"Thank you. I think that would be advisable, Inspector. Was there anything else you needed to know as time is getting on now?"

"One last thing really before we leave you to it. Did you, as a family, ever go back to your old neighbourhood once you moved to Suffolk?"

Sadness crossed his face. "I've gone back once or twice. Not had the balls to tell the rest of the family, however, in case I stirred up all the old feelings that were swirling around when Jeff disappeared."

"That must have been tough for you. Any reason why you went back?"

He inhaled a large breath. "I trawled the nearby streets, looking at folks to see if I recognised Jeff at all. I always thought he'd been abducted, you see. Hoped that he would escape his confines and run away one day."

"It's good to have hope, Mr. Ryland. Not so good when nothing comes of it, I suspect. Casting your mind back to the time he went missing, did you and your family conduct a search at all?"

"For a few weeks. Before school, after school, my brothers and I would be out there, scouring the streets and all the nooks and crannies we knew as kids. Then when Dad came home from work, we volunteered to go out with him for an hour or so. It was heartbreaking to see the old man with constant tears in his eyes. Devastating to see both our parents crumble before our eyes. All the stress proved too much for Mum to bear in the end. That's why we moved. Now all this is starting up again, and I fear she's not going to handle it so well."

Sally nodded. "I'm sorry for all the upset the family are enduring at present. Hopefully, we'll be able to offer a definitive answer as to who the victim is soon."

"Fingers crossed that happens, Inspector, for all our sakes."

"We'll go now. Thank you for seeing us at such short notice. It really is appreciated."

He walked them to the front door and shook their hands before they left.

Sally exhaled a large breath as they returned to the car. "On to the next one."

"Which one? Warren or Thomas?"

"Well, as we had the pleasure of talking to Thomas yesterday, I think we should visit Warren first. Have you got the address of where he works?"

Jack punched the postcode into the satnav while Sally started the car. The garage where Warren Ryland worked was a fifteen-minute drive away. They parked and entered the large opening to the garage.

Three men, all wearing oil-stained overalls, looked their way when they entered.

"Hi, I'm DI Sally Parker, and this is my partner, DS Jack Blackman. Is one of you gents Warren Ryland?"

Two of the men glanced in the direction of a tall thin man with sandy hair and a goatee beard to match.

"That's me. Have I done something wrong?"

Sally smiled to try to ease the man's anxiety. "Not as far as we know. Would it be convenient for us to have a brief chat?"

He grabbed an oily rag from off the engine of the car he was tending to and wiped his hands. "About anything in particular?"

Sally scanned the area. "Is there somewhere more private where we can chat?"

"There is, but it's a shit tip. I don't have any secrets from these guys."

"Very well. It's concerning your brother, Jeff."

The colour drained from his face. "What about him?" Warren shuffled his feet then leaned back on the motor he'd been working on.

"Have you spoken to your parents recently?"

"Not for a few days. Why?"

Sally thought that strange, considering the other brothers were aware of what had been found. "I see. Well, yesterday a discovery was made at the house next door to where your family used to live."

His eyes widened, and his chest expanded and deflated rapidly. "What type of discovery?"

"The owners of the property unearthed a skeleton. It's too early for us to determine who the skeleton belongs to, but the pathologist has given us a few clues to go on. The main one being that the victim was between the ages of eleven and thirteen."

Warren shook his head, and tears filled his eyes. He opened his mouth to speak, but no words came out.

"Hey, man, you okay? You look as though you're gonna puke any second."

No sooner had one of his colleagues mentioned being sick than

Warren turned his head to the side and vomited on the floor beside him.

Sally faced Jack and rolled her eyes.

One of the other men rushed to the back of the garage and returned with a sack of sand. He poured some over the vomit and placed a hand on Warren's shoulder. "Are you all right, mate?"

Warren scrubbed a hand across his face. "I don't know. I need to sit down."

Sally peered over her shoulder. "Why don't we talk outside? You can get some fresh air while you sit on the brick wall out there."

Sally walked ahead, and Jack remained behind to accompany the man outside. Once they were seated, she asked, "Are you all right, Warren?"

"I don't know. Do my parents know?"

"Yes. We visited them yesterday. Your brother Thomas also came to the house, and we've just come from your other brother's place of work. I'm surprised no one has told you. Any idea why they should want to keep this news from you?"

"I don't know. Other than they might have thought it would affect me the way it has. Is it him? Jeff?"

"We don't want to make any assumptions at this stage. However, it is looking likely to be the case. I'm sorry this has come as a shock to you. Were you close?"

"Close? He was my brother—of course we were close."

"I apologise. That was insensitive of me. Are you up to discussing what happened around the time your brother went missing?"

"What? That was thirty-odd years ago, and you expect me to remember that far back?"

"Not every detail of course, but anything you can tell us will help with our enquiries."

"I'm not sure I can. I blocked a lot out at the time and still do, if I'm honest. Jeff going missing hit me harder than the rest of the family. He was always with me, you see…"

"And he wasn't that day?"

"Yes. I mean no. Oh heck, I can't remember. My mind plays tricks on me because of the grief I felt at the time. Everything is a muddle, and I can't figure out what's the truth and what I want to believe is true. Does that even make sense? To my ears, it sounds confusing, but hey, welcome to my world. My life has been non-stop confusion since the day he went missing. My God, could this really be him? After all these years of not knowing what happened to him. Where was he found?"

"Do you remember your neighbour called May?"

"Yes, a sweet lady who cared for us occasionally. What about her?"

"The remains were found under a shed that was erected in her garden."

The colour drained from his face. "What? Are you telling me that you suspect May of killing whoever the remains belong to?"

"It's hard to discount the evidence we've uncovered. Unless some other reason comes our way, then yes, we suspect May might have been behind this."

He shook his head in disbelief. "Never, not dear May. You can't honestly believe she would be capable of doing such a dreadful crime. She loved us, especially Jeff. She had a soft spot for him because he was the youngest."

"Then perhaps you can tell us who you think could have been responsible for this, Warren?"

He shrugged and stared at her. "How should I know? This is the first I've heard of a damn body, and I'm expected to summon up a name for you?" He clicked his fingers together and added, "Just like that?"

"Forgive me. I'm asking too much of you. Please, will you do me a favour and try to think back? It could prove vital." His tanned face contorted with pain, and his brow wrinkled as he thought.

There was a silence between them for a few minutes. Sally noticed Jack getting impatient and shot him a warning glance.

Finally, Warren shook his head and slapped his hands on his thighs. "I've thought and nothing, nothing is coming to mind. I can't summon up something that is no longer there, Inspector. You're going to have to take my word on that. Grief messes with people's heads. I'm sure you're aware of that, right?"

"I am. Okay, why don't I leave you a card? If anything from around that time jolts your memory, you can get in touch with me."

"Very well. Did you ask the same question to the others? My parents and my brothers?"

"Yes. They can't seem to recall anything except searching for your brother every day at different times of the day. Do you remember doing that?"

His eyes glazed over when he contemplated her question. "Sort of. Like I said before, everything is such a blur. My whole life has been a blur, if you must know. It's only in the past few years that I've resigned myself to not seeing him again." He held up his hands to show off his tan. "I've just returned from my first ever holiday abroad."

"Where did you go?" Sally asked, envious that he'd been away.

"Turkey. A lot of my friends kept insisting what a beautiful country it is and urged me to go there. A group of them persuaded me to tag along. It was okay, I suppose. Not sure I'd go again. I'm not really one for socialising that much. All they seemed to want to do was spend every night in the bar and every day on the beach sleeping it off. I'm the type who likes to explore new places I visit, not sit in the same place all the time getting hammered."

Sally smiled. "I totally get where you're coming from. I think I'd feel the same way as you. Glad you finally plucked up the courage to go abroad. Try not to let what I've told you today upset you. There's no point letting it affect you until it has been confirmed."

"I understand. When will we be told?"

"A forensic anthropologist is working on the skull now. That might take a couple of weeks to complete. I'll ring your parents the second I hear back from the pathologist. It was nice to meet you, Warren. Should you remember anything significant in the meantime, please ring me, day or night."

The three of them stood and parted ways.

As he and Sally climbed into the car, Jack let out a large sigh. "It must have been awful for them all, Warren in particular, if he was the one in charge of Jeff. I can't imagine the guilt that man has carried on his shoulders all these years."

"I was just thinking the same, Jack. We never know what these people go through. It's hard to judge as everyone deals with their grief on a different level."

"So, what next?"

"We'll nip and see Thomas. To be honest with you, I'm not expecting him to impart any further information than what he told us yesterday, but it would be wrong for us not to drop by and see him. Perhaps something has popped into his mind since he saw us."

"Is that a pig flying past?"

Sally jabbed him in the leg. "Cynic. Let's take a wander over there and see."

Jack nodded and punched in the postcode for the bank where Thomas Ryland worked. As luck would have it, he was free when they arrived.

He welcomed them into his office and pounced right away. "What news do you have for me, Inspector?"

"Sorry to disappoint you, but we don't have any news as such just yet. We're still waiting on the specialists to carry out their roles in the investigation. We were in the area, visiting your brothers, and thought we'd drop in to see you."

"Any specific reason?" he asked, his tone abrupt.

"Not really. We're keen to see if anything has come to mind from when your brother went missing."

"Nothing other than what we discussed yesterday. Are you telling me that your investigation is reliant on what my family and I can recall?"

"No, that's not it. It was a lot to take in yesterday. It's been thirty-three years since your brother was reported missing. I just wondered if something had come to mind overnight, after a bit of the shock wore off."

"Well, it hasn't. We're still no further forward. You told us you found a body that might or might not be my brother's. There's nothing more to say on the matter, surely, is there?"

Sally was rarely lost for words, except when she came up against someone with Thomas's attitude. She'd seen the same type of look and heard the same tone in the years she had been married to Darryl. She knew when to take a step back. Rising from her chair, she extended her hand across the table. "Thank you for your time. We'll be in touch soon."

She left the room with Jack close on her heel. As she stormed across the car park, Jack grabbed her arm.

"Hey, slow down. Don't let him get to you, Sally. You're always safe with me around. I'd never let another man lay a hand on you again."

She smiled at her partner, grateful for his chivalrous nature. "I know. That means a lot to me, Jack. Let's get back to the station."

CHAPTER 9

AFTER SPENDING AN EVENING WITH SIMON, going over the Ryland case, she felt relieved when he told her the results of the reconstruction were expected by the end of the week.

Sally passed on this snippet of good news to the team as soon as she entered the incident room the following morning. The team gathered around for their morning briefing.

"Let's start with the Ryland case first. Jack and I managed to speak to all three brothers yesterday, but sadly, none of them could really shed any light on the events of what happened the day their brother went missing. They were, however, surprised by the fact that a body was discovered in May's garden. None of them had a bad word to say about the old lady. What I did pick up was that while Thomas and Shaun had got on with their lives, Warren, who was the closest in age to Jeff, has truly struggled since the lad disappeared. He was relatively quiet and, I suppose, guarded about what he had to say on the matter. I didn't push things with him. If the need arises, then Jack and I will revisit him in the near future."

The team listened and nodded at the appropriate times, and Joanna was the only one who took down notes.

"So, we move on today to question the neighbours. Joanna, do you have a list for me?"

Joanna reached behind her and placed a sheet of paper on the desk between them. "Three names—that's all I've managed to find still living in the same area, boss."

"I guess it's a start. Jack and I will visit them all this morning." She swivelled sideways towards Jordan. "How did your day pan out, Jordan?"

"It was tough, boss. I'll need another day to go over things and put them in some kind of order, if that's all right?"

Sally smiled and nodded. "Take all the time you need, within reason. I'm just glad we're working the case and that some of these families will hopefully get some closure from this. Let me know how you get on at the end of the day, if you would. I want to revisit Abbott in prison again in the next few days, if only to keep the pressure on him."

"Really? You're going to put yourself through that again?" Jack asked, tilting his head in surprise.

"I'm not about to let a deviant prick like that rattle my cage, Jack. I'm desperate to know where he's buried Katrina Hathaway, for her mother's sake."

"I get that. But the shit wants something in return. I wouldn't be happy dealing with the git on his terms. I'm surprised you're willing to buckle under the pressure."

"Not sure I'd class my intentions as 'buckling under the pressure', but I do feel the necessity to partially play along with him if it means we get the results we're after. Let's hold fire on what we feel is right or wrong for now until Jordan gives us the full facts on the cases he's looking into. Deal?"

Jack crossed his bulging arms and shrugged. "It's your call. I was only voicing my opinion."

"And I appreciate you doing that. Right, anything that we haven't covered yet?"

The team shook their heads.

"Okay, let's crack on then. Stuart, why don't you work alongside

Jordan for the day? You've finished the reports you were writing yesterday, yes?"

"I have. I can do that, boss."

"That's sorted then. Are you ready to head off, Jack?"

"Ready as I'll ever be, I suppose."

* * *

"WHAT'S TAKING THEM SO LONG?" Jack queried when they arrived back at the crime scene, which was still cordoned off.

"I should imagine SOCO are stripping all the walls et cetera in the house. I didn't think to ask Simon if his team had finished that part of their examination. I'll give him a ring now."

Jack left the car and went into the garden to see if there were any technicians on site while she placed the call to Simon. "Hi, it's me. Jack and I are back at the crime scene. You didn't tell me your guys hadn't finished yet."

"Sorry, I presumed you'd know that. These things take time. You want us to do a thorough job, right?"

"Of course. I'm just surprised that they're still here. Have they uncovered anything else at this point?"

"Not yet. They've started at the top of the house and are working their way down."

"Crap, are you saying they're ripping the place apart, Simon?"

"I'm telling you that we're doing what's necessary and what we always do when a body is found in someone's back garden."

"Shit! The poor homeowners."

"What you should be concerned about is the skeleton we found and not the homeowners, Sally," Simon said.

She was taken aback by his sharp tone. "I know that, Simon. I'm doing my best here. It isn't easy when the case is thirty-odd years old. I'll see you later." She ended the call and cringed for hanging up on him. She had never done that before and knew she would be wrapped up in guilt for days. Sally exited the car and went in search of her partner.

"Jack, where are you?" she called from the back door.

"I'm up here."

Sally wound her way through the small rooms, and he came out of one of the bedrooms just as she began her ascent up the stairs. "You really don't want to come up here, boss."

"What? Why? They haven't found another body, have they?"

"No. It's a bloody mess, though."

"Shit!" Despite his warning, Sally forged ahead. Stopping outside the first bedroom, she gasped. "Damn. What the heck? Is this mess really necessary, guys?" she asked the two technicians dressed in white paper suits. They looked as if they'd been used in a disaster zone, judging by the amount of dust and mud splattered on them.

One of the technicians removed the bulky mask he was wearing to answer her. "It's a necessary evil, Inspector."

"Surely you have equipment you can use rather than tearing all the walls apart, for goodness' sake."

"We do, and we've found a few bones in the walls. That's why we've gone the extra mile on this one."

"What? I've just rung the pathologist—he didn't tell me you'd uncovered anything along those lines."

"As it happened, the bones belonged to a few animals rather than another human."

"Oh heck. Well, that's good then," she replied sarcastically.

Jack sniggered.

Her temper flaring, Sally glared at him. "Glad you find all this amusing. I can tell you that I find it appalling."

"I'm not amused by what they found, just by your reactions. What did you expect them to find? Nothing?"

"Er...if you must know, Jack, yes! That would've been good." She turned back to the technician. "Do you think these animal bones are from the same era?"

"It's hard to judge. We've sent a few samples back to the lab for the guys to examine while we continue ripping this place apart."

Sally shook her head. She was trying not to put herself in the homeowners' shoes, but it was becoming increasingly impossible. She would be devastated if something similar ever happened to a house she owned.

"Come on, Jack. I need to get out of here." She marched back down the stairs and out into the garden, where she drew in a large breath of fresh air.

"Are you all right?"

"I'm fine. Overwhelmed by the complexity of the case, I suppose. Why would someone bury animals in the walls of a house?"

"Maybe it was a test to see if a smell emanated from the walls."

"Why? What on earth are you getting at?"

He hitched up a shoulder. "Well, the forensic guys have only just begun their search. What if the person who lived here—that May Childs, for instance—was testing her theory out on animals before she moved on to burying bodies in the walls?"

"That's insane. All right, going along with your warped theory, why would this kind lady—that's how she's been touted as by the family, after all. Why would she bury a body in the back garden?"

Jack threw his arms out to the sides. "I don't bloody profess to know the ins and outs of a serial killer's deranged mind."

"Whoa! Hold your horses, Jack. Who has labelled her a serial killer?"

Annoyed, he waved a hand in front of him and left the garden.

Sally trotted after him and yanked his arm. "Don't walk away from me. It was a genuine question that I'd like an answer to."

"You caught me out. The words escaped my mouth before I engaged my brain."

Sally sighed heavily. "You need to squash those kinds of thoughts, Jack, until any evidence comes to light."

"All right. I will. I've already apologised. What more do you want from me?"

Sally took a step back and frowned. "Some respect for your senior officer would be nice. What's eating you?"

"Nothing. Have you looked in the mirror lately?" He stormed off again and slipped into the passenger seat of the car.

Sally was in two minds whether to challenge him further or to let things lie. His behaviour was uncalled for and totally unexpected. She exhaled a breath and walked towards the car, her gaze focussed on him. His head was turned to the side as if he was avoiding her.

She sat down heavily in the driver's seat and punched him gently in the thigh. "The last thing I want or need right now, Jack, is you and I falling out."

He turned to face her. "That's the last thing I want, but why pounce on me like that?"

"I'm sorry. I said what I said without thinking. You must admit your assumption came out of the blue."

"I thought you were the type of copper who was keen on covering all the angles."

Sally tucked a stray hair behind her ear. "I am. You know better than to say that. Okay, let's forget this ever happened and get back to business, deal?"

His right shoulder hitched up a notch. "If you want. Just to make things clear, I'll be keeping my mouth shut in the future."

"What? Isn't that taking things a little too far? Borderline childish behaviour?"

"It is what it is."

She huffed out a breath and started the car. "Punch the first address into the satnav, will you?"

He glanced at her as if she'd gone mad. "Doh! It's two doors down. Are you seriously going to drive there?" He laughed, breaking the tension that had developed.

Sally doubled over with laughter and tore open the car door. "What are you waiting for then?" Once Jack was out of the car, she pressed the key fob to lock the vehicle, and together, they walked around the front of the house.

The house they intended to call at first appeared to be well maintained by its owner. The windowsills seemed to have been freshly decorated in a red masonry paint. The small garden was exceptionally tidy, considering the recent bad weather. The edges of the lawn were crisp and clean, not a stray blade of grass in sight.

Jack rang the bell. "Neat garden. The owner obviously has a lot of time on his hands."

Sally pointed at him and winked. "Great detective work, DS Blackman."

Jack tutted and shook his head. Before he could respond, the door opened to reveal a man of retirement age in a knitted tank top over a long-sleeved striped shirt and a pair of jeans with an ironed crease down the front of each leg.

"Hello, are you Mr. Donaldson?"

He frowned and his gaze drifted from Jack to Sally. "I am. Who wants to know?"

Sally produced her warrant card and introduced herself and Jack. "Would it be convenient if we came in for a quick chat, sir?"

"Is this about what's going on next door?"

"Yes, sir. Would you mind?"

He pushed the door open wide and gestured for them to come in. "There's no need to take your shoes off. Come through to the lounge. I was just having a cuppa. Can I get you one?"

"We're fine, sir. Not long had breakfast ourselves," Sally replied, speaking for both of them.

"Please yourselves. You better take a seat."

Sally sat on the couch next to Jack. "Have you lived here long, Mr. Donaldson?"

"All my life. This house belonged to my parents before me. Never moved and never had an inclination to live elsewhere. This is a decent area. Bit noisy with the kids now and then, but you switch off from that if you know what's best for you. Otherwise, they'd drive you nuts."

"I see. I'm assuming you'll remember all your past neighbours, in that case?"

"Of course. There's nothing wrong with my mind. I remember everything that's ever happened on this street. Bloody shocked at what the new arrivals dug up in their garden. Never imagined anything like that would go on around here. Just goes to show what happens behind closed doors, doesn't it?"

"Did you know May Childs well, sir?"

"Yes and no. We used to speak in the street. In those days, we knew where each other was, but we kept a polite distance until someone needed something. There was none of that mixing at social gatherings like those awful barbecues. Nothing like that. Now and then we used to meet up at the social club down the road. Of course, that's now gone, boarded up because people grew out of attending the functions. Life goes on for some folks, I guess."

"Sad, but true, sir. What about the Rylands? Did you interact with them much when they lived around here?"

"Again, we nodded hello, and William and I went for the odd pint now and then. Nothing more than that, though. His wife was really nice, doted on those boys of hers. Especially the youngest one. Well... until he ran off, that is."

"Is that what you were told had happened to Jeff?"

He frowned. "That was his name. Yes, why? Are you here to tell me that he didn't run off?" His eyes widened, and he shook his head slowly. "No! You're not telling me that what you lot have discovered is that nipper, are you?"

"We're unsure at present, sir. It's true—we have discovered some remains. Right now, all we know is that the remains belong to a child between the ages of eleven and thirteen."

His eyes narrowed as he thought. "The lad was around that age when he went missing, I seem to recall."

"He was twelve. You're correct about that. Did you have much to do with Jeff, sir?"

"Nope. I didn't get involved with any of the kids. I'm not one for spending time with the younger generation, you see. They piss me off most of the time. Demanding little critters, screaming the place down when they don't get their own way. When I think back to the way my old man used to clout me round the ear when I shouted to someone in the street. I suppose nowadays parents aren't allowed to lay a hand on their child, are they?"

"That's right, sir. It would be an offence to do so."

"Pity. You want to see the behaviour of some of the older kids around here. Smoking and drinking on the street corners. You can't tell me the bloody parents aren't aware of what they're up to. They choose to ignore it, though. Sickening, it is. There's always been gangs around here, but they've never been much trouble."

"Are you saying the gangs are becoming worse, sir?"

"Either that, or I'm guilty of being less tolerable in my old age."

Sally smiled at the old man. "So, is that how the kids in this street have always amused themselves?"

"Mostly. I suppose there's been the usual cliques here and there."

"Do you remember if Jeff and his brothers were in a gang or gangs back then? They differed in ages, which might have caused a problem."

"I think so, but don't quote me on that. I don't recall them ever being trouble."

"Glad to hear it. Is there anything else you can tell us that you can remember about the neighbourhood back then? Perhaps you can think of something that possibly didn't sit well with you that took place in the area around that time."

His head tilted. "I don't understand what you're getting at, Inspector. Apart from the lad's disappearance being odd, you mean?"

Sally shrugged. "Sorry, I was trying not to put words in your mouth and fear I've only ended up confusing you. Obviously, Jeff went missing, but do you recollect anything that seemed odd to you? Such as a stranger hanging around, acting suspicious? Anything along those lines?"

He nodded and chewed his lip as he thought back. After several moments, he shook his head. "I'm sorry, no. Nothing is coming to mind."

"That's fine. Don't worry about it. It was a lot to ask of you. I'll leave you a card in case anything should come to mind once we've left."

"You do that. I'm sorry I can't be more helpful to you. Will you be speaking to anyone else while you're here?"

"We're hoping to talk to Daisy and Frank. Our research tells us that they were also living in their properties around that time, is that correct?"

"I was just about to suggest the same. Plus, you'll be pleased to know their memories are just as sharp as mine. I think Daisy will be the best one to help you with your enquiries. I don't mean this disrespectfully, but women tend to know more about what's going on in their neighbourhood rather than us men, right?"

Jack coughed, suppressing a laugh, and muttered, "What you're trying to say in a roundabout way is that they're nosy."

Sally shook her head but found it hard not to smile. "Charming!"

Mr Donaldson sniggered. "The lad's right, you know. The fairer sex has always been...how shall I put this? Ah yes, inquisitive."

Sally smiled at the old man. "Hey, don't you start ganging up on me. I have enough problems with my partner on that score."

They all chuckled.

"Hey, but you get the last laugh and the final word, I bet, what with you being his superior officer, eh, duck?"

"I do indeed. Well, if there's nothing else you can think of, we'd better see what Daisy has to say."

"You better make it snappy. She tends to go into town on the bus around eleven every morning. Hates to be cooped up in the house for long hours during the day, that one."

"Ah, and you'd know she goes out daily, how? By seeing her go out when you're nosing out the window, by any chance?" Sally smirked.

Mr. Donaldson tapped the side of his head with his fist. "Touché, Inspector. I walked right into that one, didn't I?" He faced Jack and leaned forward to whisper, "She's sharp, ain't she?"

Sally chuckled inside and struck an imaginary finger in the air.

"Yep, so sharp she cuts herself at times," Jack admitted with a grudging smile.

Sally rose to her feet and motioned for Jack to do the same. "Okay, thank you for seeing us, Mr. Donaldson. It's been a pleasure."

The man struggled out of his chair and walked them back to the front door. "The pleasure was all mine. I can tell you're a determined woman, Inspector. I hope that determination solves this case quickly.

We're all eager to find out what the heck has been going on under our very noses. If you get what I mean?"

"I do. Thank you for the compliment. My team and I will strive to do our best, the same as we always do. Enjoy the rest of your day."

"I will. Thank you."

CHAPTER 10

THEY LEFT and walked next door to the house that belonged to Daisy Meadows. Jack did the honours of ringing her doorbell. The garden at the front of the property was pretty, with a vast array of rose shrubs that were in bud, about to make an appearance once the sun had worked its magic on them.

A lady with a friendly chubby face and a warm smile opened the door. "Hello there. I take it you're the police, come to question me about what's going on at May's old house. Am I right?"

Sally smiled as she thought over the conversation they had just had with Mr. Donaldson regarding the woman's inquisitive nature. "You're right, Mrs. Meadows."

She held her right arm up and wagged her finger. "That'll be Miss Meadows. Never married, dear. Never felt the necessity as I've always been self-sufficient. Had a good job when I was working. PA to a top solicitor in my day."

"Were you? Good for you. Would it be all right if we come in for a quick chat? I'm aware time is marching on and that you go out every day at eleven."

The woman rolled her eyes, a faint smile forcing her ruby-red lips apart. "He's a card, that one. He has the audacity to call me bloody nosy. I suppose he doesn't look in the mirror that often. Cheeky devil, he is. Sorry, come in. I've just popped the kettle on if you're interested in a cuppa, or aren't you allowed to accept if you're on duty?"

"A coffee would be great, if you're making one," Sally replied, stepping into the house.

"Come through to the kitchen. I think it's tidy enough for visitors. If it isn't, I apologise in advance. I tend to do my housework in the evening. Can't stand watching all the drab programmes on the TV nowadays. Soap after bloody soap, and when they're not on, the screen is full of talent shows. Who wants to listen to screaming kids singing? It's beyond me at times. Set in my ways, that's my trouble. Let me flick the switch and prepare the cups. Fire away with your questions if you want."

"Not many questions as such, more an enquiry into what you remember from thirty-three years ago. Oh, I'm DI Sally Parker, by the way, and this is my partner, DS Jack Blackman."

"Oh damn! Now you're going to slap me on the wrist and tell me off for not asking to see some form of ID before I let you in, aren't you?"

Sally smiled and shook her head. "It's so easy to become distracted. You're safe with us. I can show you our IDs if you want to see them. However, I would urge you to be more cautious in the future."

"Easy mistake to make. Not that anything bad ever happens around here...hmm...in light of why you lot are around here at the moment and the forensic team, maybe that was the wrong thing to say. I'm not doing too well today so far. Shall we start over?"

Sally and Jack both laughed with the woman.

"Why don't we do that? How is your memory, Daisy?"

She filled the cups with hot water, stirred the drinks then handed a china cup and saucer to each of them. She invited Sally and Jack to take a seat at the small pine kitchen table. The kitchen hadn't been updated in years, but it was spotlessly clean. "My memory is perfect. What do you need to know?"

"It would be good if you could tell me a little about what life was like back in eighty-five."

She pulled out a chair and sat. "Help yourselves to sugar." She pointed at the sugar cubes in the bowl on the table. "Now, how shall I describe it? I suppose I would say it was a lot friendlier back then. Now you're going to pull me apart and say even though a skeleton has been dug up in someone's garden, aren't you?"

Sally shrugged. "It seems the most logical question to ask next. Did you know your neighbours well back then?"

"I wouldn't say that well. Being a spinster, I tended to be out at work all day during the week, and at the weekend…well, I spent most of my time catching up on the chores. You know, the boring stuff, like cleaning and ironing et cetera. The weekends had a tendency to fly by compared to the working week. Why is that?"

"Nothing has changed in that respect, I can assure you. Did you ever get the chance to play catch-up with your neighbours over the weekend?"

"Sort of. Those I wanted to mingle with were really nice. There was the odd idiot living around here back then who I steered clear of."

Sally motioned with her head for Jack to take notes. He withdrew his notebook and flipped it open to a clean page.

"Can you remember their names?"

She rubbed at her chin for a few seconds. "There was a builder living across the road from me. One day, he would smile at me. The next, his eyes used to dart daggers in my direction. What was his name now? He died a few years back. Oh wait…yes, Bill Drake."

Sally inclined her head. "The same builder who erected May Childs's shed?"

Miss Meadows shrugged. "I wouldn't know what he got up to while I was at work during the day. Funny bugger. Borderline arrogant, I'd class him at times. Not sure why he would look down his nose at some of us. His house was always in a state. The worst bloody one on the street. I'll point it out to you when I show you out. Like I've said already, he's dead now, so someone else owns the house who treats their property with more respect than he ever did. Funny that. You'd think he would've had the sense to maintain his own property well to attract business."

"I'm with you on that one. Do you think May had used this man before?"

"I really wouldn't like to say. I'd hate to lead your investigation up the garden path, Inspector."

"I appreciate that. We'll delve into Mr. Drake's background when we get back to the station, just to make sure. Note that down for me please, Jack."

"Will do."

"Can you tell me what it was generally like in the evenings around here, Miss Meadows?"

"Please, call me Daisy. It was a mixture, really. Sometimes, it was peaceful, and other times it could be noisy."

"Noisy? Any specific reason for the noise?"

"Mainly because of the exuberance of the gangs messing around."

"Ah yes, we've heard about the gangs. Did you ever have any bother with them?"

Daisy's mouth turned down at the sides. "Can't say I did. I remember telling one of them to get out of my garden when one of their balls came over the hedge once. Apart from that, nothing as such. Has someone told you differently?"

"Not really. Can you tell us how many gangs there were?"

"Two, I believe. One filled with younger boys, up to the age of fourteen or so. The other from fourteen upwards, into their late teens. I don't think you could ever consider them bad lads, not like the youth of today. They were just rowdy now and again. I remember the boy who went missing, Jeff Ryland. He belonged to the younger gang while I believe two of his brothers were involved in the older one."

"Interesting. Anything else you can remember about them?"

"I seem to think one of the gang members was a relative of May's. He stayed with her on the odd occasion."

Sally slowly turned her head sideways to glance at her partner. Jack raised a knowing eyebrow in return.

Facing Daisy again, Sally asked, "Can you remember his name?"

Daisy stared at her cup for a moment or two. "I believe it was

Steven. Sorry, can't for the life of me think of his surname. I do know it wasn't the same as May's, if that helps."

"It does. We'll investigate that. Did he stay at the property often, do you know?"

"Again, I'm not really sure. Hang on a second… Yes, when poor May passed away, he came to the house. I had a brief chat with him to pass on my condolences. He was grateful, said that the family were grieving badly for May and that the house was going to be put on the market."

"By the family or by him? What I'm trying to ask is, who the house was bequeathed to in her will. Any idea?"

"Him. He did tell me that. Said he was cleaning the place up and looking around it had stirred up fond memories of the time he'd spent at the house with his dear aunt."

"That's helpful. We'll be able to find his surname going down that route then. You're doing well. At last I feel as though we're getting somewhere. Do you know if this Steven is local?"

"Wouldn't like to say. Wish I could confirm that, but I can't. I suppose he must be if he tidied up the house before the sale went through."

"Was he in the older gang or the younger gang?"

"Definitely the older gang. I believe he used to hang around with one of the middle Ryland boys, if that makes sense?"

"Was it Shaun or Warren?"

"Now you're asking. Truthfully, I used to get mixed up with all their names."

"That's not a problem. We're in touch with the Rylands; we can ask them. I asked your neighbour the same question. Do you recall anything going on around then that you possibly regarded as suspicious at the time?"

Her mouth twisted as if she were chewing on the inside of her cheek. "Not really. It was a small friendly community with a few days of loutish behaviour thrown into the mix periodically."

"Honestly, what you've told us already has been a great help."

Daisy sipped at her drink. "It's awful to think that no one knew what they were living next door to. I know you probably can't tell me, but I'm going to ask the question anyway. The body or skeleton, there's a rumour going around that it could be Jeff. Is it?"

Sally heaved a large sigh. "This isn't me being awkward, but at this stage, we're not sure. We need the pathologist department to give us those details. As you can imagine, it's much harder for them to identify a skeleton rather than a victim that is still intact."

"I can see how difficult that must be for them. It'll probably take months to identify the body. Am I right?"

"Hopefully, it won't be too long. An anthropologist is in the process of reconstructing the head for us now."

"That must be interesting work. I watch a lot of true crime on the TV—when I can be bothered to watch it, that is. It amazes me how accurate these reconstructions can be. Isn't science wonderful? It's come a long way over the years since DNA was developed."

"It certainly has. Right, we have another neighbour we need to check in with before we go back to the station. I'll leave a card in case anything else comes to mind." Sally pushed the business card across the table towards Daisy.

"Thank you. Sorry I couldn't be more help. You see, back then, once I got home from work, I closed the curtains and shut out the rest of the world. Not every day, of course, just now and then." She smiled. "I know what you're thinking. What about the reputation I have for being a nosy parker? Well, what else am I going to do with my time now that I'm retired?"

Sally laughed and stood. "Too right. I think I'm going to take a leaf out of your book when I retire, too. We'll both make up for lost time."

"Exactly. Glad we're on the same page. Of course, on a more serious note…I'll keep my fingers crossed that you find out who those bones belong to and help to put a family's life back on track once again." She gasped. "Oh Lordy, I've just had a dreadful thought."

"What's that?" Sally asked.

"You don't think May had anything to do with what they've dug up, do you?"

"It's an avenue that we're keen to delve into. It does seem strange that the body was buried in her garden just before the shed was erected. Of course, we haven't had confirmation regarding that yet. So it's pure speculation on our part."

"Goodness. Well, if you put it like that…oh my, it's like something out of a horror movie."

"Most crimes like this invariably are. Fact is always harder to stomach compared to either fiction or what the producers like to portray in films."

"Isn't that the truth, reading some of these ghastly stories in the newspaper? There appears to be so much hatred in this world. I dread to think what it must be like being a serving police officer these days."

"Thankfully, we're lucky around these parts. I suppose it's only a matter of time before that changes and the criminals get tired of causing havoc in the big cities and try their hand in the more rural communities."

Daisy shook her head. "That's a terrible prospect. Hopefully, I'll be long gone by the time things get that bad."

Sally shrugged, and Jack got to his feet. "I suppose we better get going. If you should think of anything else, don't forget to ring me."

"I'll show you out. I do hope the investigation goes without a hitch for you. It would be nice to know whoever was buried in May's garden has a proper burial soon."

They shook hands at the door, then Jack and Sally left the house.

"She seemed a nice lady," Jack noted.

"She did. Both she and Mr. Donaldson seemed nice. I hope our luck stays with us when we question the third neighbour."

"It's good that we've discovered a family member link to May, though, right?"

Sally nodded. "You bet. Let's see what Frank Wallis has to say then get back to base to do some digging about this relation. I must say, it's definitely piqued my interest."

"Mine, too." Jack pushed the gate open to the next house and walked up the path ahead of Sally. He rang the bell, and they waited a while until the homeowner came to greet them.

A bald man opened the door. "Yes?"

"Hello, sir. Are you Frank Wallis?"

The man nodded.

"We're DI Sally Parker and DS Jack Blackman from the Norfolk Constabulary. Would you mind if we come in and have a chat with you?"

He pointed at the SOCO van in the road behind them. "This is about that, isn't it?"

"It is."

He sighed heavily. "You better come in then. Not that I'll be able to tell you much." He turned his back.

Sally rolled her eyes at Jack then entered the house.

Mr. Wallis showed them into a small tidy lounge at the front of the house. The furnishings were dated but in good condition. Sally sensed the man had a wife caring for him.

"So, how do you think I can help you?"

"According to our records, sir, you've lived at the same address for over forty years. Is that correct?"

"Yep, this was our first home when we got married. Turned out to be our only home to date. Freda loves it around here. Me, not so much. I stay here to keep her happy. That's what we men do, right, lad?" he replied, bringing Jack into the conversation.

"Yes, it's always good to go down the happy-wife-equals-happy-life route, sir. Saves a lot of grief in the long run," Jack agreed, smirking.

"Do you remember the lady who owned the house?"

"May Childs. Yes, of course I do. She was one of my customers. Everyone around here was, in fact."

"Customer? What did you do back then?"

"I was the local milkman. They're a rarity nowadays. We used to do a lot for the community. Some of us were taken for granted, but mostly, people appreciated the service we provided. I used to get the odd note left in a milk bottle, people asking me to let the dog out into the garden at a certain time or to take their washing in if it was raining."

"Are you serious?" Sally asked, amused and amazed by his statement.

"Too right I'm being serious. You know what? Most of the time I bent over backwards to ensure their wishes were met." He shrugged. "It's the way the world worked back then. This, well…I can tell you, it's bloody shocked the life out of me. All right, that's a bit of an exaggeration because I wouldn't be speaking to you today if that were the case, but you get my drift."

Sally smiled. "I do. Can you tell us what kind of woman May was?"

"Friendly and down to earth. She'd do anything for you. I remember her watching me read one of the notes a neighbour had left me with some chore written on it, and she asked if everything was all right. I explained that Mrs. Smith wanted me to take her prescription into the doctor's by a certain time that day, and I said I couldn't possibly do that without getting behind on my rounds. The boss would have killed me if I finished too late. He didn't mind me doing the odd saintly act but objected if I did too much to help my customers. May was kind enough to volunteer to collect the neighbour's pills for me."

"I can understand that from his perspective. What about anyone who visited May, perhaps stayed with her occasionally?"

His gaze drifted over to the window. "Well, there was always her nephew around these parts. I can't really tell you if he stayed there or not. I suppose he must have done now and again, because he belonged to one of the gangs around here."

"Any idea where his parents lived?"

"Sorry, no. I couldn't tell you. He was round here frequently, so I'm guessing they didn't live that far away. Mind if I ask a question of my own?"

"Go ahead."

"You seriously don't think May could have done this, do you?"

"The truth is we're unsure what went on at present. Hence the need for us to conduct house-to-house enquiries. Fortunately for us, you, Daisy and Doug were all living around here during the same period. We're hoping any information you guys can give us will help solve the case. So far, all we've managed to find out is that May was a lovely person. Hardly the type of person to have bones buried in her back garden. Are you sure you can't recall anything bad about her?"

His eyes narrowed. "No, not that I can think of. I'm sure if anything bad had happened, it would be embedded in my mind. There's nothing there. Sorry."

"Okay, don't worry. Daisy and Doug both mentioned the gangs that were prevalent at the time. Did you have any major dealings with them? Conflicts of sorts, anything like that?"

"The odd run-in with one or two. They were cheeky buggers really. Nothing too heavy, like throwing bricks through the window or running a key down the side of someone's car. I wouldn't class them as 'gangs', as such, not compared to the ones that are causing havoc today. I'd say they were just a group of lads meeting up to have some fun. Nothing more than that. Oh wait, I tell a lie...it's all coming back now. There were a few instances around that time when the older gang got into bother. Damn, what was it they were up to? Let me think about it for a second or two."

Sally and Jack glanced at each other.

Frank clicked his fingers. "I know...they started robbing a few of the shops in the town. Of course, all that stopped when that lad went missing."

"Jeff Ryland?"

"That's the one. His brothers used to be in the older gang. When the boy didn't come home, they started searching for him at every opportunity. Out there day and night, they were. Some of us lent a hand when we could, but mostly William, the father, was eager to do the searching on his own, as though it was his responsibility to find the boy. He was in a terrible state after the first week had elapsed. Nearly on knees, he was. I tried to comfort him, but he was having none of it. If anyone spoke negatively about the boy's disappearance, he'd jump down their throats. He was sure the lad had been abducted by someone rather than think of him as running away from home. Jesus, if what you lot have uncovered at May's house turns out to be Jeff...well, it really doesn't bear thinking about. Do the family know?"

"Yes. We had the unfortunate task of telling them yesterday. Of course, we've yet to make a formal ID, which should be on the cards soon enough. Were you surprised when the family moved away from the area?"

His head tilted from side to side. "Yes and no. It must have been a wrench for them. I know the mother was in a terrible state. Every time I spoke to her, she used to plead with me to keep an eye out for him on my travels. Of course, that went without saying. I always did that anyway. I remember feeling useless for not being able to do more for the family—we all did. To witness so much pain and suffering— well, no one should experience that amount of upset in their lives. I thought it was brave of them to move away. I suppose they always knew that if Jeff turned up, that one of us would take him in and get in touch with them."

"It does sound like a fabulous community to be involved in. The incident must have affected you all."

He ran a hand over his face. "It did. Finding the bones has ensured my nights are restless now, too. It's the guilt. It's hard to bear. I know the bones haven't been identified yet, but come on, Inspector, you don't have to be a genius to figure out that's going to be Jeff you've discovered."

"We're keeping an open mind at present. It's important for us to build a picture of what went on in those days, and we're delighted with the information we've gleaned so far."

"I'm glad to hear it. The lad deserves a proper grave to rest in, if it is him. I don't envy your task, though. Who on earth would do that to the lad? Not May, surely. I just wouldn't believe that in a million years."

"All right, if not her then who else? Was there anyone hanging around at the time? A stranger in the area, acting suspicious?"

He contemplated her question for a moment or two. "I honestly can't remember anyone fitting that description, and that has nothing to do with my brain cells dying off. I think something like that would have stuck in my memory. We didn't put up with shit of that nature years ago. I remember my daughter saying there was a strange man lingering at her school gates one time, and I drove down there like a shot. Sorted the pervert out, gave him a good hiding down an alley. He never returned to watch the kids again, I can tell you."

Sally covered her face with her hand. "Gosh, I really wish you hadn't told me that, Mr. Wallis."

Jack sniggered.

Frank Wallis seemed confused. "What? Oh right," he said, when the penny finally dropped. "I know I was in the wrong, but bloody hell, no one likes to think of their children not being safe at school, do they? I was carrying out a community service."

Sally dropped her hand and smiled at the man. "Commendable of you but also very much against the law. I'm going to pretend I didn't hear that part of the conversation. So there was someone hanging around. Was it at the same time Jeff went missing?"

"Not really. This occurred a good few months later. That's why I hit the roof—the thought of my daughter going missing like the lad…"

"I see. I can imagine it was a tough situation to find yourself in."

"Hey, I think I would have reacted the same way," Jack added.

Sally looked his way and shook her head. "Not helpful, partner."

He shrugged, and his head dropped down to his notebook once more.

"Getting back to the Rylands. They doted on their children. Did you ever see another side to their nature where the kids were concerned?"

"I have to say no. Never. They idolised those children. Maybe that's why they moved—to protect the other boys after Jeff went missing. Although he was the youngest, of course. I always felt the older boys were more than capable of defending themselves adequately enough. I know the other young lad…crikey, what was his name?"

"Are you talking about Warren?"

"Yes, that was it. I think he took his brother's disappearance really badly. He used to be an outgoing kind of lad but went into his shell."

"We've spoken to him. He told us that he felt responsible for not taking proper care of his brother around that time. He's come to terms with it now, but only in the last five years or so."

"Poor lad. Not sure how I would have felt if this type of thing had happened to me and my brothers when we were growing up."

"Okay, is there anything else you can tell us that you think we should investigate?"

"There really isn't. I think you'll be barking up the wrong tree if you think May did this, though. Of course, I'm not a detective, but I did know the woman personally."

"Thank you. That's reassuring to know. We'll leave you to it. Thank you for taking the time to answer our questions. All right if I leave you a card?"

"I was going to ask you for one. You know what it's like—something you see on TV will jolt a memory. I'll be in touch if that should happen. It goes without saying that I wish you luck going forward. Are you going to do one of those appeals?"

"We're going to see where the information we've been given leads us first. Thanks again for your help. Stay there. We can see ourselves out."

"Nonsense," he said, bouncing out of his chair as if he were thirty years younger.

After leaving the house, they returned to the car. Sally's phone vibrated in her pocket and she fished it out. It was Simon. "Hey, you. What news have you got for me?"

"I'm keen to update you on what's going on. The anthropologist just rang me to say that he's almost finished the reconstruction. I thought you'd want to know right away."

"That's brilliant news. When will it be completed, love?"

"Tomorrow at the latest."

"Great news. That'll mean we'll be one step nearer. Sorry for hanging up earlier."

"Don't ever apologise. My team said they had found some bones in the walls that belonged to animals."

"I know. Sounds bizarre to me. Do you think the person who buried the skeleton in the garden had thoughts of burying the person in the wall, perhaps? A trial run?"

"Seems likely." He let out a huge sigh. "All this case is doing so far is raising more questions. I can understand it being so frustrating for you."

"Thanks, I appreciate your understanding. If that's all, we're about to head back to the station. I'll see you later."

"That's all for now. Be in touch if anything else rears its head."

Sally ended the call and returned the phone to her pocket. "Right, let's get back and spend the afternoon digging. I sense we're getting close to a conclusion on this one, Jack. I wonder how Jordan and Stuart are getting on with the other case."

"There's only one way to find out."

She started the engine, took another look around the small estate then drove off. Her thoughts lingered on what they had learned regarding the gangs.

CHAPTER 11

SALLY AND JACK returned to the station, bearing goodies in the form of rolls and cakes for the rest of the team. After eating lunch, Sally instructed Jack to find out what he could about May's nephew via the woman's will.

She sat down to speak with Jordan and Stuart concerning what they had managed to find out about the Hathaway-Abbott case.

Jordan placed a sheet of paper in front of Sally to browse. He then went on to inform her that after speaking to the family members they could find, of both the missing girls and the girls who were murdered by Abbott, he and Stuart had drawn up a map of the area showing where each of the girls had last been seen.

Sally studied the map. "Hmm...so that's an area of around—what? Eight to ten miles?"

Jordan nodded. "You've got it, boss. As suspected previously, it looks like he used to go out at night and prowl the area, searching for his victims. A lot of the girls were likely picked up after they had been out for the night with friends."

"In other words, you're saying they were more than likely drunk?"

"Exactly. I had a sneaky peek at the PMs of the murdered victims who were found within a day or two of their abduction, and yes, there were faint traces of alcohol in their system."

Sally tilted her head from side to side. "There's another possibility to that scenario, of course—that Abbott offered them drink, while he had them in his care, shall we say?"

"Absolutely. A couple of the parents said that Carina Sanders and Sophie Johnson mentioned to their friends that they thought they had seen a man following them once or twice."

Sally raised an eyebrow. "Interesting, which leads me to believe he targeted the girls and perhaps followed them until the opportunity arose to snatch them."

Jordan and Stuart both nodded.

"That's my take on it, boss," Stuart replied.

"The previous incidents, did he stalk them on nights out or on their way to or from work?"

Jordan flicked through his notebook then said, "A mixture of both."

"How far away was Abbott's house from this area?"

Jordan tapped the map with his finger. "Abbott's house is here. Therefore, slap bang in the middle of the area he cruised."

Sally paused to think for a moment. "Shame we didn't have the use of satnav technology back when he was arrested. We'd probably be able to trace where he was using as a base to keep the girls."

"It's still a pretty big area, boss, but if you give me and Stuart a few days, we could begin an in-depth search of the area."

Sally chewed on her bottom lip until it hurt. "I just think that would be a waste of resources, to be honest. Chances are that if he used a derelict house or somewhere along those lines before he was arrested, his hideaway has probably been demolished or renovated by now."

Jordan nodded. "Maybe you're right, knowing how much regeneration has taken place in the area in recent years."

"What type of reaction did you get from the parents?"

"We spoke with the parents of the girls whose bodies haven't been located up to this point. We told them we were looking into the cold cases and hoped to have some good news for them soon regarding their daughters' whereabouts. We tried not to raise their hopes too much. Not sure if we succeeded on that front, though, boss."

Sally sighed heavily. "It's a tough one. Exactly the same as what Jack and I are dealing with on the Ryland case. Okay, where do we go from here? I'm thinking I should take another trip back to prison to grill Abbott again."

"If you think that will help, boss," Jordan said, shrugging.

"I've got a suggestion," Jack called over.

"Go on, surprise me," Sally replied, swivelling in her chair to face him.

"I was thinking, after having another coffee, we could shoot over there and perhaps call in to see the nephew on the way back."

Sally's interest spiked. "Are you saying that you've located him?"

Jack grinned smugly. "Was there any doubt I would?"

"Not from me. Where does he live?"

"Between here and Norwich."

Sally nodded and thought over the prospect of coming face to face with the lowlife Abbott again. She rose from her chair. "Let me contact the governor, see if he'll give us permission to see him this afternoon, and we'll go from there. Good work, guys. I'm proud of what we've achieved so far today."

She settled into her chair, opened the small address book on her desk and located the governor's number. She placed the call.

Governor Ward's secretary put her through after a brief pause. "Hello, Inspector Parker. How are things going?"

"Hello, Governor Ward. Hit and miss, truth be told. I was wondering if you would grant me another visit with Abbott."

"I don't see why not. When?"

"Would this afternoon be too soon?"

"I can arrange that. What time were you thinking?"

"How about four, give or take a few minutes?"

"Excellent. I'll let them know on the gate to expect you. I have to say that since your last visit, Abbott has been surprisingly quiet. Reflective even, according to the officers on his wing."

"That's interesting to know. Do you think he's going to break down and tell us where the girls are buried?"

"Who knows? Let's just say it looks like your visit touched a nerve. Maybe it's a good idea that you're coming this afternoon, if only to keep up the pressure."

"That's brilliant. Okay, I'll gather a few things together and jot down some notes I want to ask him and head over there. Would it be all right if my partner tagged along?"

"I don't see why not. I might not be around when you arrive. I have a meeting mid-afternoon that could possibly be a lengthy one."

"Not to worry. Hope to catch up with you another time in that case. We're bound to be back and forth a few more times yet, if Abbott has his way."

The governor laughed. "I fear you could be right on that count, Inspector. These guys enjoy nothing more than toying with the police."

"Hopefully, I have enough ammunition to shoot down any attempts he might have of doing that. My team have been working exceptionally hard on his case and have come up with some surprising facts."

"Good to hear. Shame it's taken yet another team to work the case to obtain results. I'm sure the families of his victims will be eternally grateful to you if you can figure out what's happened to their daughters."

"It's galling. However, once my team and I get involved, there's usually only one conclusion. I hope that doesn't come across as sounding too conceited?"

"Not if it's the truth. Good luck, Inspector. If all goes well, perhaps you'll give me a quick ring in the morning to update me on your progress."

"That's a deal. Sorry, one last question before I go. Has Abbott ever seen a psychiatrist?"

Governor Ward sighed. "Several. I think the last count off the top of my head was four."

"Oh wow! Okay, thanks for that. Speak soon." She hung up, and still smiling, she returned to the incident room to give Jack the news. "Yep, we're on for this afternoon. We'll set off from here at about ten to three. The governor is allowing us to visit Abbott at four o'clock. If we estimate an hour interviewing Abbott and then get back on the road, we'll drop in on May's nephew on our way back. It could be a late one, Jack. You might want to pre-warn that lovely wife of yours."

Jack picked up the phone on his desk. "On it now. I'll get the post-code for Jay's address. Hopefully, he's not one for necking a swift pint down the pub before he ventures home for the evening."

"Do we know if he's married?"

"Not sure."

"Joanna, would you mind looking into that for us, please?"

"My pleasure, boss. I should have the information for you soon." The sergeant immediately bashed the keyboard in front of her, making Sally smile.

"Let me know. I'll be in my office, preparing a few questions I want Abbott to answer. I hate to admit this, but I think I'm going to take a few crime scene photos with me."

Jack shook his head and glared at her.

"Don't give me that look, Jack. It's just in case we need them to persuade him. Although, saying that, the governor has just informed me that Abbott seems reflective since my last visit. I'm hoping I won't have to use the photos. We'll see how things go when we get there."

Jack reluctantly nodded. "Okay, I get where you're coming from, in that case."

"Thanks for giving me your permission, matey," she said, marching into her office. She decided to ring Simon while she had a spare five minutes in case it slipped her mind later on in the day. "Hi, it's me. Quick call, not work-related. Well, I suppose in a way it is."

"Get to the point, Sally. You're not the only one with a busy sched-ule," Simon replied jokingly.

"Sorry. Usual thing. The brain is working at a hundred miles an hour. I'm going to be late home tonight."

"That's a coincidence. So am I. How late?"

"Probably be home around seven. Why are you going to be late?"

"Just heard about an accident on one of the B roads near here. A woman and her child were knocked down by a speeding car at a zebra crossing."

"Shit! I hope they got the driver?"

"Yep, I believe so. You might see me at about nine."

"Want me to cook something?"

"Either that, or I can drop by the local pub and order a couple of meals to bring home."

"What? I didn't know they did takeaways."

He chuckled. "They don't. I used to drop in there on my way home when I had to work late. I'd order a meal, they'd plate it up, and I'd drive home and drop the plate back to them the following day."

"Nifty. And there was me thinking you were totally self-sufficient when you were a single guy."

"I was, kind of. Anyway, I've got to love you and leave you. Oh, I forgot to ask. Why are you going to be late?"

She inhaled a large breath. "I'm going back to the prison to see Abbott."

"What? Do you really need to do that?"

"Simon, I've told you not to worry about me. If it puts your mind at rest, Jack will be accompanying me. Then we're going to stop off en route to question someone regarding the other case we're working on. It's all go around here this week, I can tell you."

"You work too hard. Make sure you keep the weekend free for some me-and-you time."

"I'm hoping it'll work out that way. Mum and Dad are expecting us on Sunday as usual, though. Hope that's all right?"

He tutted. "Of course it's all right. Looking forward to it. See you later. Love you."

"I love you, too. Enjoy the rest of your day…um…you know what I mean." She laughed and hung up.

Jack appeared in the doorway with a cup of coffee in his hand. "Thought you might need another one of these. I've cleared things with Donna, and Joanna has located a marriage certificate for Steven Jay."

"Thanks, Jack. Good work all around, eh?"

"I reckon. Let's hope the visit to the prison goes according to plan. Am I going to be there when you question Abbott?"

"Of course you are. Don't you want to be?"

"I'm in two minds about it. You might have to restrain me if he starts using bloody mind games on us. You know I can't abide turd brains who do that sort of thing."

"You need to keep control on that temper of yours when we go, matey. These guys have nothing better to do than sit in their cell, churning over in their tiny brains what will be the best way to wind us up. The trick is not to let them think they're winning."

He flapped a hand in front of him. "I know all that crap. But knowing it and not reacting to it when placed in that situation are two entirely different matters."

"Just try. For my sake and for the sake of the families we're trying to help, okay?"

He nodded and left the room.

Sally sipped at her coffee and noted down the questions she intended to ask Abbott. Then she sorted through the case file and extracted the crime scene photos of one of the victims, Karen Pitts. She was the victim whose body had deteriorated the least when a walker had stumbled across her in a boggy area.

She inserted the photos in a new manila folder, along with the details Jordan had researched about his other likely victims, plus the map of the area the two sergeants had come up with. She slipped the list of questions into her notebook. Then she left the office to collect Jack. He was sitting at his desk waiting for her to emerge. "Are you ready?"

"I am. I've got the details of Jay's address et cetera here."

He held up his notebook, and Sally nodded. "Okay, team, thank you for all your hard work today. Leave at five if you want to, and we'll meet up again in the morning. With any luck, we'll have several pieces of important information we can share with you after our afternoon trip."

CHAPTER 12

SALLY AND JACK went through the scanners at the prison then followed the guard to the same room where Sally had interviewed Abbott a few days before. She inhaled and exhaled a few large breaths as they awaited the man's arrival.

"Are you nervous?" Jack asked.

She faced him and smiled. "Yes and no. I hate being back here because of what's gone on in the past. I guess I'm a tad anxious more than nervous. Shh...I can hear the clanking of chains. He's on his way."

The door opened. Abbott paused at the doorway when he spotted Jack.

The prison officer behind him gave him a slight nudge to get him moving again. "Come on, Abbott. We haven't got all day."

Abbott scowled at the officer then shuffled towards the small desk. "Who's he?"

Sally smiled briefly at the prisoner. "My partner, DS Jack Blackman. Do you have a problem with him being here?"

"As long as he keeps his big mouth shut, we should all get on well. Have you got them?"

Sally pretended she didn't have a clue what he was referring to. "Sorry? Have I got what?"

"Nice try." He started to stand, but the officer behind clamped a hand on his shoulder and forced him back in his seat.

"Stay there, Abbott."

"I told you. No photos, no information," he sneered.

Sally shrugged and flipped through the file. The motion didn't sit well with her, but she passed the photo across the desk to him. His eyes widened, and he spent the next few moments staring at the photo from different angles, wearing an infuriatingly large smile. Bile rose in her throat, and Sally thought she was going to be sick. Jack nudged her under the table with his knee, and she nudged him back, letting him know she was all right.

"Well? You've got what you wanted," Sally said. "Now it's your turn to pay up. Where is Katrina Hathaway's body?"

He roared, and his head dropped back against the officer behind him. The officer shoved Abbott's head forward again and shrugged at Sally.

"Thanks for this. Is it mine to keep?"

"Just tell us what we want to know," she replied tersely.

"Ooh…touchy bitch when you want to be, ain't ya?"

Jack slammed his clenched fist on the table. "Answer the damn question, you sick bastard."

Sally grinned when Abbott's gaze latched on to hers, but inside, she was seething at her partner for breaking his promise not to overreact.

"Easy, tiger. I'm surprised at you, Inspector, for not training him properly. Or did you tell him to grin and bear everything I said, and it's a case of him showing an ounce of insubordination?"

"Not at all. He's his own person. I tend to let my team members think for themselves."

His gaze intensified, appearing to search deep into her soul. "Is that right?" he challenged, tilting his head.

Sally nodded. "Fact. A deal is a deal. Where did you bury Katrina Hathaway?"

He sat back in his chair, glancing from Jack to Sally and back again. He folded his arms. Time wasting, Sally suspected.

"Now which one was she? Ah yes, I remember—the cute one with the blonde ringlets, am I right?"

Straining to keep her cool, she agreed. "That's right."

He scratched his head, a puzzled expression on his face. "She could be in either of two places. The first is…"

Jack had flipped open his notebook. Abbott's gaze landed on his pen. Jack glanced up at the man. Abbott locked eyes with him, toying with him.

Sally nudged Jack's leg under the table, and out of her peripheral vision, she saw him drop his challenging gaze back to his notebook. "Okay. I knew this would be a waste of time. Let's go, Jack," Sally pushed her chair back and stood, her attention never leaving Abbott's eyes.

Jack closed his notebook and followed suit, much to Abbott's amazement.

"All right, all right. Man, you guys need to be able to read when someone is trying to wind you up by now."

Sally and Jack both sat again. "Do you think it's appropriate to mess with us over this? Is winding the police up what turns you on these days?"

"I have to have some pleasure in life, Sally. Now that beautiful women like you are out of my reach." He peered over his shoulder at the officer behind him then leaned over the table. "Of course, the officers take it in turns to visit my cell at night for extra curriculum activity, if you get my drift."

The officer placed his hand to his head and screwed his finger into his temple. "Bullshit!" he said, clearing his throat to shift what Sally assumed was an imaginary tickle.

Abbott smirked. "He's bound to say that, right? He's the one who visits me the most in the dead of the night."

Sally shook her head. "If you're trying to shock me, nothing—I repeat, *nothing*—you could ever say will do that."

"Is that so? Maybe I should go into detail of how each of the women reacted before I finally ended their miserable lives. Because they were, you know, miserable."

"They told you that, I presume?"

"Oh yes. They easily came to me because they were all searching for something to enhance their lives. I was happy to oblige. I showed them what it was like to be loved by someone. I did love them, if only for the briefest of moments. I loved them intensely until they took their last breath. The girls would have gone to their maker knowing what true love was, if only for a few minutes in their lives. I have a generous soul and giving nature inside." He held his hand up to his chest.

"It would be generous of you to tell us where Katrina and the other girls are buried."

"Let's talk about the other girls for a second or two, shall we?" A small smile pulled his thin lips apart.

"What about them? We know who the others were. We've worked it out for ourselves."

"You are a bright spark. Was it you, or was it one of your minions, like Jack here?"

"Actually, it was another member of my team. It didn't take them long to figure out who the other victims were after spending time looking over the information I gleaned from you on my last visit."

He grinned. "I knew you were a smart cookie. All the male officers they've sent to see me over the years were egotistical bastards who thought they'd get the information out of me through being angry. They were wrong, as they found out to their cost. I like you, Sally. I can see into your soul. I recognise a woman who has suffered at the hands of a man. He was wrong to treat you like that. I would have shown you what true love could feel like, if we'd met before I got sent down."

Trying hard not to react, she held his gaze. "Maybe, but then you would have killed me, just like you did to the other girls you fell in love with."

"See! I told you you're smart. A darn sight smarter than the psychiatrists who've spent hours visiting me over the years, too, I hasten to add. Most of them didn't have a clue. Again, I found myself only warming to the woman. I have an affinity towards the female gender. What more can I say?"

"While you're warming to me, perhaps you'll tell me why you changed your MO?"

He frowned. "My MO? Ah, yes—Lynn Jackman. She may have only been ten years old, but when I picked her up, she'd been at her friend's house playing dress-up, which made her appear a lot older. I actually thought she was sixteen, if not slightly older. Can you imagine my shock when she whispered her real age to me when we were having sex? I killed her there and then. Can't abide people who intentionally lie to others, can you?"

Sally shook her head in disgust at Abbott's blasé manner and hypocrisy. "Why didn't you simply drop her off somewhere? Perhaps if you had, you wouldn't have been caught. You were arrested when they found her body in the boot of your car, am I right?"

"You know damn well you are." His anger was evident in his tone. "The truth is, I panicked. Kidnapping her was the biggest mistake in my life. No—correct that. Getting caught was the biggest mistake."

"Now you have the chance to make amends. Tell us where the girls are: Sophie Johnson, Millie Potter, Carina Sanders and Jasmine Winkleman. You loved and killed them all, didn't you?"

His chin dropped to his chest, then his watery gaze met Sally's again. "I did. The trouble was, none of them could find it in their hearts to love me back. No one—*no one* makes a fool of me like that."

"I sense a bit of remorse in you since we began this meeting. Won't you find it in your heart to tell me where the girls' bodies are buried, not just Katrina's?"

He gulped noisily. "After all this time, the novelty has worn off. I had control at one time, keeping the information to myself, but now, what does it matter? I'll tell you."

Sally's heart rate escalated tenfold. "I'm waiting."

"After you've given me more photos to look at." Sally shuddered at his laugh.

"You're sick. We'll find them." She produced the map from the file and placed it in front of him. "We know your hideout has to be in this area; we're not stupid." She watched his eyes scan the map and settle on a certain area on the Norfolk coastline.

I've got you, you bastard. You might think you've won this round, but you're grossly mistaken, arsehole!

She snatched the map and the photo back and tucked them in the folder again. "I'm going to give you one last chance to reveal all."

"That sounds like a threat, Sally."

Despite cringing when he uttered her name, she pulled back her shoulders. "It was. I'm giving you one last chance to tell us. If you give up the location, I'll do my best to have a word for you with the governor to get you extra privileges. On the other hand, if we discover the bodies ourselves, then I'll make sure you stand trial again for each of their murders. Proper trials, not Mickey Mouse ones, which will ensure you spend the rest of your life behind bars."

"It ain't going to happen, Sally. You'll never find the girls. And if that's the case, they'll always belong to me."

Sally rose from her seat. "This meeting is over. We will find them, and when we do, you have my assurance that I'll come after you again. You've had your chance to do the right thing, and you blew it. I'll ensure you never obtain your freedom. Ever."

Jack stood and followed Sally to the door.

They left Abbott doubled over in laughter.

"Fucking sick shit!" Jack mumbled as they retraced their steps through the corridor to the exit of the prison.

"I agree. Fucking scumbag. I'm even more determined to find those girls now. I think I know where they are, too."

Jack halted and stared at her. "How could you possibly know from what he's just said in there? I didn't pick up on anything."

"I watched his eyes carefully when he studied the map. They were drawn to an area on the coast Wells Next the Sea. I'll get Jordan and Stuart to search the area in the morning. I have a good feeling about this, Jack. The bastard dropped his guard for an instant and screwed up."

"Well, I didn't notice anything like that. Let's hope you're right and that you're not about to send the boys on a wild-goose chase."

Sally let out a weary sigh. "I feel drained. Let's hope our next stop proves to be just as successful."

CHAPTER 13

"I THINK we're in luck. Looks like he's home." Sally noted the time on the dashboard; it had just turned five forty-five.

Steven Jay's home stood on a small new-build housing estate on the A11 at Ketteringham. It was a large house with a double garage. Two cars were parked on the drive.

"Great news. No hanging around, and we get to go home earlier than anticipated. That's music to my ears."

"And a little presumptuous on your part. Come on, grouch."

They approached the house as a neighbour was parking his car in the drive opposite. He paused, watched them for a moment then slipped the key into his front door. After another glance their way, he closed the door.

"Inquisitive lot," Jack grumbled.

"Ignore them. Our concern lies with Steven Jay, no one else." Sally rang the bell, which chimed melodically on the inside of the house.

Within minutes, a man in a grey suit opened the door.

"Hi, are you Steven Jay?" Sally asked, smiling.

"I am."

She extracted her ID and introduced herself and Jack. "Would it be possible to come in for a quick chat?"

"In connection to what? Oh, wait a minute. If it's about the accident on the main road, I arrived after the incident took place. I didn't see the accident as such."

"It's not about that, sir."

"Then what is it about? I've just come home from a hectic day at work. This is the last thing I need to contend with this evening."

"It's regarding a matter to do with your childhood, sir. We shouldn't keep you long."

He shrugged and gestured for them to step inside the house. "Come through to the kitchen." He led them into a large kitchen-diner, where a blonde woman, considerably younger than Steven, was stirring ingredients in a wok.

"Steve? Who's this?" the woman asked.

"This is my wife, Gail. This is the police, love. Any chance you can put dinner on hold for a spell?"

Gail's eyes grew large. "Of course. What do they want?" She immediately switched off the stove.

"I've yet to find out. Is Daniella all right? Maybe you should go and check."

"Okay, I'll be back in a second."

Gail left the room, and Steven invited Sally and Jack to join him at the large oak dining table. "What's this about exactly?"

Sally removed her notebook and turned to the page in which she had jotted down the notes from the three older neighbours on the Rylands' former estate. "We're investigating something that was found at the property that used to belong to your aunt May."

His expression changed instantly from inquisitive to horrified. "What's that supposed to mean?"

"Sorry. What I meant to say is that a few days ago, we were called to your aunt's former residence after a skeleton was discovered in the back garden."

His hand covered his face. "A skeleton? How did that get there? Sorry if that's a dumb question."

Sally nodded. "An understandable question, I would say. One that I was hoping you could help us answer."

The hand covering his face dropped to splay across his chest. "Me? How do you think I can help? My aunt died in that house over five years ago. I'm not sure how many people have owned the property since then. Have you asked them about this?"

"There was no need to do that, sir, as the remains were buried during the time your aunt owned the house."

"What? How do you even know that?"

"Forensics, sir. You can obtain a vast amount of detail using the science."

He fell back in his chair. "What does this have to do with me?"

"As I said when we arrived, this visit is to do with something that occurred during your childhood. When speaking to the neighbours still living in the area, your name cropped up a couple of times."

"It did? In what context?"

"Do you remember being part of a gang along with the Ryland brothers, sir? They lived next door to your aunt."

"Not particularly, no. Why?"

"Did you ever visit your aunt's house?"

"Of course I did."

Sally nodded. "Did you ever stay in the residence overnight?"

"Yes. Why?" He shuffled forward in his chair and scratched his neck.

"How often?"

"A few times a month. I'm not sure. We're talking thirty-odd years ago. My memory from back then isn't so good."

"I appreciate that, sir. Have you had a head injury in recent years?"

He appeared puzzled by the question. "What kind of question is that?"

"It's just that the elderly neighbours recalled things in detail, and yet a much younger man like yourself seems to be having problems."

He inhaled a large breath then let it out slowly. "Perhaps they've led uneventful lives and like to dwell on the past. I don't. My childhood wasn't a very happy one, Inspector, and I've tended to block it out of my mind over the years."

"I'm sorry to hear that. Your mother was raising you by herself, I seem to remember."

"She was. I stayed at Aunt May's when Mum had to do a night shift. Is there a law against that?"

"No, sir. There's not. While you stayed at your aunt's, you used to hang around with a group of boys, didn't you?"

"If you say so, although I can't really recollect that happening." His gaze dropped to his hands, which were clenched together on the table in front of him.

"So you don't remember the day Jeff Ryland went missing?"

He lifted his head to look at Sally. "Vaguely, I think."

"Vaguely? But you used to hang around with his brothers in a gang. Didn't you help in the search when he was reported missing?"

His chin fell against his chest again, and Gail entered the room.

"What's this about, Steve? Are you going to be long?"

"Something from my past that I'm having trouble recalling, love. Nothing for you to worry about. I don't think we'll be long now, will we, Inspector?"

"That depends, sir. Can you answer the question?"

"I might have helped in the search, possibly."

"Surely something as significant as a child going missing would be hard not to remember."

"What? A missing child? Steven, what is she talking about?" Gail asked, shocked. She sank into the chair next to her husband and reached for his hand.

"Let me fill you in, Mrs. Jay. Back in May nineteen eighty-five, a neighbour of Steven's aunt May went missing. He was twelve years old at the time. His body was never recovered, and according to his family, nothing has been heard from Jeff Ryland since."

Gail stared at her husband. "Did you know this boy, Steven? You've never told me about this."

"Nothing to tell. Life was a roller coaster back then. I was shunted around all over the place. Forced to make new friends every time we moved."

"Is that why you don't have a clear image of what happened

regarding Jeff?" Sally asked, feeling sorry for the man for the first time since they'd stepped foot in the house.

"Maybe. I chose to block a lot of things out when my father left us. He used to beat the crap out of me."

Gail gasped. "Why didn't you tell me that?"

He smiled at his wife. "Would you have wanted to get involved with someone so damaged?"

"What a ridiculous question. Of course I would."

Sally cleared her throat. "Sorry, just a few more questions, and then we'll be out of your hair. Forensics have been at your aunt's former house and discovered more bones in the walls of the house. Any idea how they likely got there?"

His eyes narrowed for an instant, and he gulped noisily. "No idea. What type of bones?"

"We're waiting for confirmation, but we believe they are remains of animals. Did your aunt ever have any animals?"

He shook his head and shrugged. "Can't remember."

"That's a shame. Perhaps you can tell us what your relationship was like with your aunt? Did she ever lay a hand on you?"

"No! Never. She was a lovely lady. Why would you ask such a question?"

"Because someone buried that body in her back garden. If it wasn't her then maybe you can offer a suggestion?"

He heaved out a long breath. "Maybe it was the builder who erected the shed for her."

"Maybe. It's an avenue we're investigating at present. Okay, thank you for all your help. If we have any more questions, we'll drop by and see you again, if that's all right?"

"I hope you find out who the bones belong to, Inspector. I'll show you to the door. You might also want to check about a lodger that Aunt May used to have living with her around that time, too."

"A lodger? Do you remember his name?"

He shook his head. "Sorry, I can't."

"Not to worry. We'll do some digging. Here's my card if you should think of anything you'd like to add."

"Good luck," he said then gently closed the door.

Walking to the car, Sally craned her neck when raised voices came from the Jays' kitchen. "Oops, looks like he's going to cop an earful tonight for keeping secrets about his past."

Jack peered over the roof of the car. "Yep. There's nothing worse than you women feeling left out when we forget to tell you things."

"Get in the car. And don't package all women in the same way, Jack."

"Okay. Sorry," he apologised, a suitably remorseful expression on his face.

* * *

SALLY DROPPED Jack off at the station and continued on the journey home to Simon's house. She still struggled calling her new living accommodation her 'home'. *That time will come in the future, I hope.* Everything was so new to her at the moment. She yawned a little during the drive. It had been a long day yet again. Upon reflection, it had also been super frustrating in parts.

Simon was getting out of his car when she entered the drive. He crossed the gravel to greet her, wearing a large smile. She felt a pang of guilt for hanging up on him earlier on in the day. She exited the vehicle, and they shared a kiss.

"I'm sorry."

He took a step back and stared at her. "For what exactly?"

"For ending one of our calls on a sour note. It's been a day riddled with frustration."

He wrapped an arm around her shoulder and steered her towards the house. "I've got a surprise for you."

She stopped halfway across the drive. "You have?" She glanced down at the large brown envelope in his hand and tried to snatch it.

"Oh, no you don't! You'll have to wait until we're inside, you eager minx."

Sally upped her pace and reached the front door before him. She fiddled with her bunch of keys and after finding the right one let them into the grand house.

Simon closed the door behind him and handed her the envelope.

She tore it open and gasped loudly. Tears instantly misted her eyes. She dabbed at them with the sleeve of her jacket and continued to stare at the photo.

"It's him, Sal."

"My God. So it is. That's a remarkable resemblance. There's no doubt about it now. The Rylands are going to be beside themselves when I share the news. I'll have to go round there in the morning. Damn!"

Simon slid an arm around her waist and pulled her close to him. "It's going to be tough on them, and you. Let's try and forget about it this evening."

Sally smiled and slipped the black-and-white photo back in the envelope. "Agreed. Although I need to ring Jack before I do anything else."

"You do that, and I'll sort something quick out for dinner."

"You're a wonderful man, Simon Bracknall."

"I know. Omelette and chips do you?"

"Wonderful," she said, punching Jack's number into the phone as Simon disappeared into the kitchen. "Hi, Jack. It's me."

"Sally. Is everything all right? You haven't had an accident, have you?"

"No, it's nothing like that. I do have some news for you that I wanted to share right away."

"Which is?"

"Simon has just shown me a picture of the reconstruction. It's him, Jack."

"Damn. Glad it's confirmed, but I know what lies ahead with the family now. This is going to be bloody traumatic for them."

"See you at the station in the morning. We'll have a quick meeting, and then we'll shoot over to see the parents to share the news."

"Maybe we should ring one of the brothers, arrange for them to be there when you break the news."

"Good idea. I'll ring Thomas before I call the parents. Enjoy the rest of your evening, Jack."

"You, too, Sally. Thanks for letting me know."

She hung up and drifted into the kitchen, deep in thought.

"Hey, are you all right?" Simon asked, breaking into her thoughts.

"Yeah. Jack wasn't that surprised when I told him." She blew out an exhausted breath and fell into a chair at the table, which Simon had already laid for dinner. She reached for the glass of wine he'd poured and downed half of it in one gulp. "God, I needed that. Can I help?"

"Nope. I'm just waiting on the chips to brown a little, and then I'll dish up. You deserve that glass of wine by the looks of things."

"Yep. Jack and I had a relatively hard time at the prison with Abbott. He tried playing his usual tricks with us again, but I think I got the upper hand on that one."

"In what way?" Simon shook the chips in the deep fat fryer and placed the omelette pan under the grill.

"I showed him a map of the area where he'd stalked the girls. I watched him carefully and noticed his eyes were drawn to one specific part of the map. It was only briefly, but I spotted it, nonetheless. I'm going to get two of my team on it in the morning. I'm determined not to let this bastard have the final say on what happens to those girls, if only for Katrina's mother's sake. This looks yummy," she said when Simon put her dinner on the table mat in front of her.

"I hope so. Enjoy. Be careful of the spice in there. I dotted around some chorizo."

"Hmm...I don't think I've ever tasted that before. You're definitely opening up my eyes with all these weird and wonderful dishes you keep knocking up for me."

"You're worth all the effort, not that I did much tonight. Cheers! Enough shop talk now. Eat up."

Sally raised her glass to him then tucked into her delicious meal.

CHAPTER 14

"JORDAN AND STUART, I'd like you to go to this area of the map and begin searching for any likely hideaways Abbott might have used before he was caught. It could possibly be a house, a shack or shed. Perhaps even a cave along the coast there. Just be vigilant, and if you have to try and think the way a serial killer would go about things, then so be it."

"Yes, boss. That's quite a big area you've mapped out there. Any chance we could get some backup to join us?" Jordan asked.

"I'll see what I can arrange with the desk sergeant. Jack and I will be leaving soon to break the unwelcome news to the Rylands. Joanna, when we met up with Steven Jay last night, he dropped a hint that May Childs used to have a lodger. Will you do your best to try and find out who that was?"

"What? He couldn't supply the name?"

"No, unfortunately not. I'm wondering if the person could be on the electoral roll for around that time."

"I'll do my best to find him, boss. A quick question—did any of the older neighbours mention the lodger when you interviewed them?"

Sally thought back. "Actually, I don't believe they did. Do your best this morning for me."

"I will."

"I'll just grab a coffee to give me some inner strength before I call the first person on my list. Be ready to set off soon, Jack. Oh wait, no, my first call should be to the desk sergeant. I'll get back to you in a second, guys."

"I'll get the coffee," Jack offered, earning himself an appreciative smile from Sally.

After making a quick call downstairs and receiving an affirmative from the desk sergeant that he was willing to supply two uniformed officers to help Jordan and Stuart in their search, she dipped back into the outer office to let them know. "You're good to go, lads. Have a word with Pat on your way out, and good luck. Ring me with an update when you can."

"We'll do that, boss," Jordan replied.

Jordan and Stuart left the incident room. Sally collected her coffee from Jack, who was standing at the door to her office, and closed the door behind her. Taking several sips of the hot sweet drink, she inhaled and exhaled a few breaths to calm her nerves, then she reached for the phone again. After looking up Thomas's mobile number, she rang it and waited patiently for him to answer.

"Hello. Thomas Ryland."

"Hi, Thomas. This is DI Sally Parker. We met the other day."

"I remember," he replied sharply. "What can I do for you?"

"I have some news for you and your family. Obviously, I need to tell your parents first and wondered if you wouldn't mind being there when I tell them."

"It's him… It's been confirmed now, hasn't it?"

Sally sighed heavily. "I'm sorry. Yes, it's Jeff."

Thomas fell silent on the other end of the line. Sally didn't say another word until he expelled a sigh of his own that matched the depth of hers.

"Poor Mum and Dad. I have no idea what this is going to do to them. When do you want to do this?"

"I'd like to drop by this morning to inform them, preferably."

"What? Ten o'clock? Would that suit you?"

"Perfect. Will it be just you there, or will your other brothers be there, too?"

"I'll ring them, see how they're both fixed. You can count on me being there. I've got a meeting around that time, but I'll postpone it. This is far more important."

"I'll see you then."

"Thank you for getting us a prompt answer on this, Inspector. It means a lot."

Sally's heart lifted at the man's surprisingly kind words. "You're welcome. This is just the beginning, Thomas. We will find out who did this to your brother, I assure you."

"I believe you. I've been impressed with how you've gone about things so far. See you at ten." He hung up.

Sally wiped away a stray tear that had slipped down her cheek.

Why does life have to suck so much at times?

She set about the task of tackling the day's post, but it proved pointless. All she could think about was how she was going to break the devastating news to Jeff's mother and father.

She glanced at her watch and realised the time.

Damn, we better get a move on. We have an hour's drive ahead of us.

Jack turned her way when she exited the office. "We better shoot off, Jack. I told Thomas we'd be there at ten."

Jack shot out of his chair. "Talk about cutting it fine. Do you want me to drive?"

"What are you insinuating? That I'm slow?"

"No! Well, maybe. You'll have enough on your mind as it is. I'd like to help if I can."

Sally threw him the keys to her car. "You're a smooth talker at times. See you later, Joanna. I take it you haven't found anything yet?"

"That's a negative. Good luck."

"Thanks. I can't say I'm looking forward to doing this. However, with Jack by my side, I know anything is possible." She winked at Joanna, who stifled a giggle while Jack just seemed confused.

* * *

FIVE MINUTES BEFORE TEN, thanks to Jack's nifty driving, they arrived at the Rylands' family home. Thomas was waiting for them on the doorstep. He shook their hands and invited them into the lounge. Warren, Shaun and their mum and dad were all sitting down. They all seemed surprised to see them.

Sally smiled at them all. "Hello, everyone. Thank you all for coming."

"What's going on?" Shaun asked.

"Listen to what the inspector has to say, Shaun," Thomas suggested.

Janet Ryland, who was sitting on the couch alongside her husband, clung to his hand when he gave her a bewildered, lost look.

"What's going on, love? Who is this lady?"

"You remember, William. It's the nice inspector who visited us the other day. Let's listen to what she has to say, dear. Nice and quiet now."

"Okay, dear. I'm still none the wiser."

Sally nodded a thank you at Mrs. Ryland and cleared her throat. "It is extremely hard to tell you this, all of you. Last night, I received the confirmation that the remains found next door to your old house are that of your son and brother, Jeff."

The room fell silent, except for the poignant sound of Janet's sobbing.

"What is it, dear?" William asked in a dazed state.

"How do you know it's him?" Shaun asked.

Sally produced the photo of the reconstruction and handed it to him. All the brothers gathered around to view the picture. Then Thomas took the photo from his brother's hand and showed it to their mother. She gasped and traced the outline of her dead son's face with her shaking finger.

Warren excused himself and left the room, his colourless face a telling sign that he was in shock. Sally motioned to Jack for him to go with Warren to ensure he was all right.

Jack returned a few seconds later and gestured that Warren had been sick upstairs in the bathroom. Her heart went out to him. Sally scanned the room, taking mental notes of how each family member had accepted the news. Unsurprisingly, Janet seemed the most affected. William sat there, baffled by all that was going on around him. Thomas, who had heard about the news earlier from Sally, seemed almost relieved, as if he had accepted it, while Shaun kept shaking his head in confusion.

Warren entered the room a few moments later, wiping his mouth on a tissue. "I'm sorry. Are you sure this anthropologist didn't see the photo of our brother and just make it up?"

"That's not how these things work. It's definitely Jeff, and the DNA samples match," Sally replied.

"What happens now?" Thomas asked, taking a seat on the arm of the sofa next to his mother.

"The investigation has been ongoing. We returned to visit your old neighbourhood yesterday and spoke to the neighbours who still own properties there. They told us a few things that we're sifting through now. We also visited a friend of yours last night who might have given us another lead to go on."

"A friend of mine?" Thomas replied, pointing at his chest.

"Well, not just yours. I believe he used to be in a gang with the rest of you. Steven Jay. Do you remember him?"

Thomas and Shaun nodded, and when Sally turned to gain confirmation from Warren, he sank into the chair and buried his head in his hands.

"Everything all right, Warren?" Sally asked.

Jack fidgeted on the spot beside her.

"Warren?" Thomas prompted, concerned.

Warren glanced up at his brother and shook his head, tears welling up in his eyes. Sally noted the way his brothers turned to look at each other, seemingly puzzled by their brother's reaction.

"Warren, is there something you need to tell us?" Sally urged, getting a bad feeling about what was unfolding.

"It was a mistake," he muttered. "A dreadful mistake."

Before either Sally or Jack could react, Thomas left his seat and grabbed his brother around the throat. "What was a mistake? What are you talking about? You didn't? Tell me you didn't kill our brother?"

Warren tried to remove his brother's hand, but Thomas refused to let go.

Jack stepped forward and did it for him. "Let's remain calm about this, Thomas. Let Warren explain what's going on."

Thomas stood next to Shaun, who appeared to be equally shocked. Sally's heart went out to Janet and William, who were staring open-mouthed at their son.

"Warren, do you want to do this here or down at the station?" Sally asked.

"Here. My family need to know the truth. I've had to live with the guilt all these years."

"Okay, I'm going to have to ask the rest of you not to react in any way. Otherwise, I will be forced to take Warren to the station for questioning. If he's willing to tell you what went on, then I think you should all take the time to hear it from the horse's mouth. Please remain calm." Sally moved to stand next to Warren, and Jack stood on the other side.

Warren inhaled a deep breath then let it out slowly. "It was an accident. You have to believe me."

"Just tell us in your own words. One thing I have to ask you is, had Steven Jay anything to do with this?"

Warren nodded. "Yes, he killed Jeff. It was him—he did it. But I've held on to the secret all these years. Lived through the guilt of knowing what Jeff suffered at his hands, hiding those details from you. You can't imagine what it's been like for me to live through this nightmare."

"Sick bastard," Thomas mumbled. "How could you do this to Mum and Dad?"

Warren shook his head. "You don't understand. I thought it was for the best. I never imagined that his body would be discovered, not in a million years."

"Okay. Enough of the self-recriminations. Please tell us why you think your brother's death was an accident," Sally insisted.

"Jeff was walking home from school one day. The gang we all used to belong to were in the town. They were planning on hitting a couple of the shops."

"What are you talking about? We never did shit like that," Thomas claimed.

"Neither you nor Shaun were there that day. Fletch let the power go to his head and wanted to up the gang's profile. I think Jeff walked past at the wrong moment. Steven Jay thought Jeff overheard our intentions and told tales on Jeff. Fletch ordered 'Ginger', as Steven was known back then, to give Jeff a good hiding."

"Wait, you were there and didn't speak up for Jeff?"

"I couldn't. You know what would have happened if I'd intervened," Warren replied, his voice rising a couple of octaves.

"Jesus Christ, you call yourself my brother? I don't know you at all," Thomas said, flinging his arm out in disgust.

"Please remain calm, Thomas. Carry on, Warren. What happened next?"

"Ginger and I took Jeff down an alley, and Ginger laid into him. Jeff went down like a sack of spuds. Ginger started kicking him in the stomach and in the head. That's when I jumped in and told him Jeff had suffered enough. Jeff wasn't moving. I checked his pulse and realised he was already dead. We both panicked. Ginger wanted to run off and leave Jeff there, but I couldn't do it. We discussed the matter in a crazed way. Wondered if it would be better to throw him in the river or something along those lines, then Ginger—sorry Steven—came up with a solution to our problem. He said that his aunt was having a shed erected and the builder was going to be laying the foundations the very next day."

Sally thought this over for a second, and something Steven had said clicked into place. Her eyes widened, and she looked over at Jack. His brow furrowed. She shook her head and mouthed, "I'll tell you later."

Warren continued. "We waited until it got dark and moved Jeff's body. We buried him. I said a prayer over the grave."

Shaun put his thumb up and shouted, "Way to go, Warren! That was fucking decent of you."

"Please, please let him speak, boys," Janet pleaded.

"That's it. The next day, the builder did his bit. I was so relieved when we moved house. The thought of living next door...well, it was hard enough dealing with the guilt when we moved away. It would have been devastating if I'd had to stare at that shed all day long, knowing the truth."

"Do you even frigging realise how twisted that sounds, Warren?" Thomas shouted, his face red with rage.

"I know. I'm sorry to have put you all through this. I truly am."

"Inspector, I think you should remove this man from my house now," Janet said quietly.

Warren stared at his mother. "Mum, please, forgive me."

Janet shook her head. "Don't ever call me that again. You're no son of mine. How could you? Get him out of my sight, please, I'm begging you."

"I agree," Thomas said.

"So do I," Shaun concurred.

Sally nodded at Jack. "Put the cuffs on him, Jack, and read him his rights. I'll be out in a moment."

Jack and Warren left the room. At least Warren had the decency not to say anything more to the family he had devastated.

William asked his wife, "Those men were nice, love. Will they be coming back to visit us soon?"

Janet patted him on the hand. "No, love. I doubt it."

"Did you know, Inspector?" Shaun asked.

"I have to say this has come as a complete shock to me. Although, upon reflection, when we visited Warren at his place of work the other day, his reaction seemed a little suspicious. The same could be said about Steven when we dropped by to see him last night. I'm so sorry you had to witness that. I hope you think I did the right thing by allowing him to make his confession in front of you all."

"We understand why you did it, Inspector, and appreciate the work you have tirelessly put in on the case. We'll be eternally grateful. What will happen now?" Thomas asked, his shoulders slumped.

"I'll bring Steven Jay in for questioning with a view to charging him with your brother's murder. Warren will have to be charged as an accessory and will probably have an additional charge of perverting the course of justice thrown at him."

"I hope he rots in prison," Shaun said, dropping into the chair Warren had just vacated. "What a sick fucker he is! Putting us through all that pain and misery all these years. Watching us go out and search for our brother daily, when all the time he knew it was a useless exercise. I never want to see him or hear his name mentioned as long as I live."

"He'll be punished for his sins. Are you all right, Janet?" Sally asked, concerned that the woman hadn't said anything since her son had left the room.

"I will be once I bury Jeff. When can we do that, Inspector?"

"I'll have a word with the pathologist and have an answer for you by the end of the day."

"Thank you. Without you getting involved in this case, we would be none the wiser about this and still living with a murderer in our midst. Oh, I know he didn't cast the kick that killed Jeff, but in my eyes, he's just as guilty as the man who carried out the odious deed. All these years, he's known, and not once has he hinted...I can't think about him any more. My priority lies with the family who have supported me through the guilt all these years. Poor William, he hasn't got a clue what's happened. He's having one of his bad days, as you can see."

"I'm so sorry it's turned out this way for all of you. I need to go now and make an arrest. I'll be in touch later, as promised."

Thomas showed Sally to the door and shook her hand with both of his. "I—we really appreciate all you have done for us, Inspector. Do all you can to ensure Warren doesn't get away with this. It would kill my mother if he were to walk free from the sins he's committed."

"I can guarantee he won't escape punishment. Speak soon."

Sally's phone rang before she reached the car. "Hi, Jordan. Go on, make my day even better and tell me you've discovered Abbott's hideaway."

"We have, boss. I've notified SOCO, and they're on their way."

Sally slouched against the car. "Bloody hell. I was only joking. Where was it?"

"An old hut on the beach down here."

"Well done, the pair of you. Are you going to stay down there until SOCO arrive?"

"That was the plan, boss, unless you want us to return to base?"

"No, stay there. Congratulations. We've cracked this case, as well. I'll tell you all about it later. We have a couple of arrests to make in the meantime."

"Sounds cryptic. Glad you've been successful, boss. See you later."

During the drive back, Sally placed a call to the station to ask the desk sergeant to arrange for Steven Jay to be brought in for questioning. She interviewed him for two hours solid until he finally broke down and spilled his confession, even admitting that he used to torture and kill the cats that strayed into his aunt's garden—which he later buried in the walls of her house. He was arrested and thrown into the cell next to Warren's until transport could be arranged to ship them out to the remand centre where they would sweat it out until their trial dates came around.

Before she left work that evening, Sally also called the governor at the prison to share the good news. He informed her that he would take great delight in telling Abbott they had successfully discovered the bodies of his victims.

Next on Sally's list of people to call was Simon. "Hello, love. Good news. We've arrested two people for Jeff Ryland's murder. The family want to know when his body will be released. They're eager to give him a proper burial."

"That's great news. Who did it?"

"One of the brothers' friends. Plus one of the brothers had known all along and hid the secret for years."

"Jesus, really?"

"Yep. The family are naturally beside themselves. When will Jeff be released, love? I have another couple of calls I need to make before I leave tonight."

"I can arrange for the funeral parlour to pick up the remains tomorrow."

"Excellent news. I'll let them know now. See you soon." She ended the call and immediately rang Thomas to tell him the news.

Then Sally nipped out of the office to grab another coffee before she made her final call of the day. "Hello. Is that you, Miranda?"

"It is. Sorry, I don't recognise the voice. Who is this?"

"It's DI Sally Parker. I have some news for you."

"Oh gosh. Please let me sit down first." Sally heard a chair scrape on the floor. "Okay, I'm sitting. What news?"

"It's yet to be confirmed, but two of my officers believe they have discovered the hideout Abbott used, and yes, they've uncovered some bones."

"Oh God. I'm not sure how to react. I'm relieved beyond words, but I can also feel my emotions of loss rising at the same time. When will you be able to give me a definitive answer?"

Sally reflected on the Ryland case and how long the results had taken to come through. "Should be within a couple of weeks. I hope you don't think I'm jumping the gun by telling you this early."

"Not at all. I'd rather know. Can I ask you to rush things through? I had an appointment with my specialist today, and his prognosis has altered. He's given me four weeks to live."

Tears sprang to Sally's eyes. "I'm so very sorry to hear that. Leave it with me. I'll do what I can for you. Take care. I'll be in touch soon."

Sally hung up and found herself overwhelmed with emotion. Jack walked in a few minutes later to find her slumped over her paperwork, sobbing. He rushed around the desk and threw a clumsy arm around her shoulders to comfort her.

EPILOGUE

TWO WEEKS LATER, and with yet an additional cold case solved, the DCI was standing in the incident room, congratulating the team on their phenomenal success over the past month. It was no mean feat successfully solving three huge cases in that time. Sally waited for the punchline to happen, but the DCI surprised them all by giving them an extra day off.

"Thank you, sir. That's very kind of you."

"You'll need it to get everyone up to Scotland in time for the wedding." DCI Green smirked. "I take it my invitation got lost in the post, Parker."

Sally cringed at the heat burning her cheeks. "Umm...sorry, sir. I didn't think you'd want..."

He raised a hand to silence her. "I was joking. Go, all of you, with my blessing. I have a question first."

"What's that, sir?"

"Will you still be Parker when you come back to work after your honeymoon?"

"To be honest with you, sir, I'm still debating that."

"Let me know when you get back from the Maldives. Ha, it's all right for some. The Algarve is more in line with my pocket."

"Simon insisted on paying as a wedding gift, sir."

"Quite right, too. You have a decent man on your hands there, Inspector. Treat him well."

Sally chuckled. "Yes, sir, if that's an order."

"It is. Be happy and enjoy your day." He leaned forward and pecked her on the cheek.

Sally held her hand against her face where he'd kissed her long after he'd left the incident room.

"Bloody hell, Sal, the man has a heart after all," Jack whispered.

The team roared.

"Right, you heard the boss. Let's get out of here. Is everyone sure of where to catch the coach in the morning?"

"Don't you worry about us. You get off, and we'll see you up there around lunchtime tomorrow. What time is the wedding again?" Jack grinned.

Sally thumped him in the arm. "Don't even joke about that, matey. Safe travels everyone. Thank you all for coming on this trip. It means a great deal to have you all there with us."

"It's not like we're footing the bill, boss. Let's be fair," Jack shouted as she raced into the office to collect her bag and jacket.

Sally said another tearful farewell and left the station with tons of congratulations ringing in her ears from the colleagues unable to join her on the big day.

She made her way home to Simon's house. Her parents and Dex arrived a few hours later. The immediate family had decided to drive up to Scotland a day earlier than everyone else. They set off at three that afternoon and took a leisurely drive north, stopping for a light supper at a quaint restaurant in the Lakes before they continued on their journey to the guest house where they were booked in.

* * *

THE FOLLOWING DAY, Sally and her mother were adding the finishing touches to her ensemble when there was a knock on the door to the room at the guest house. Her mother opened it and gasped. "Good Lord. Lorne Simpkins, how the dickens are you? Come in, love. You're looking fit and well."

"Hello, Janine. Hey, it's Warner now, but I'll let you off. Where is she?"

"Here I am. Oh, God, I swore I wouldn't cry today, and then you walk in the bloody room."

Sally flew into her old friend's arms.

"Hush now. Don't you go getting any mascara on my two-hundred-pound suit." Lorne chuckled.

"Really, it cost that much? It's stunning." Sally said, admiring Lorne's teal suit.

"I bought it for my best friend's wedding."

"You didn't have to go to that expense on my behalf, Lorne."

"I didn't. I was talking about Katy. Lord knows when that will be."

Sally was taken aback for a moment until Lorne burst out laughing. She swiped her friend's arm. "You always were a big tease. I'm over the moon you and Tony could make it. Is Katy holding the fort?"

"Yep, she's warned me not to be late on Monday morning because she'll be eager to hand the baton back to me."

"She is funny. You'd be lost without her, though, right?"

"I would. Hey, enough about work. How are you feeling?"

After her mother left the room and slipped into the bathroom, Sally said, "I'm petrified."

"Of going through the wedding ceremony? It'll be a breeze. Over and done with within half an hour, I should imagine. Not that I've had any experience of attending a wedding of this nature. It's a beautiful setting, though, love."

"It is. No, the whole marriage thing. I keep asking myself if I'm ready to be tied down again."

"Crikey! It's a bit late to be having second thoughts, Sal."

"See. I don't know if I am or not. I love Simon to bits, but…"

Lorne grasped the tops of her arms. "But what?"

"What if he changes? Like Darryl did. I couldn't cope if Simon started to abuse me."

Lorne shook her head. "He won't. He's not the type, love. Take my word on that. If you back out now, you'll regret it for the rest of your life. You have to learn to trust that not all men are the same. If I'd thought that when my marriage ended, look at the joy and happiness I would have missed out on."

"But Tony adores you. You only have to see the way he looks at you."

"You're missing so much if you can't see the adoration that Simon has for you, Sal. Don't have regrets or dwell on the past. Put that all behind you and enjoy your beautiful day and what lies ahead of you. Simon is one in a million, just like Tony is."

They hugged again.

The door to the bathroom opened, and Sally's mother emerged. "Did you manage to talk some sense into her, Lorne?"

They all laughed.

"I might be getting on, Sally, but I'm not deaf—or stupid. Lorne's right. Simon is the total opposite to that other lowlife you married."

"All right. I feel like I'm being ganged up on now. I love you two."

"Good, then listen to us and do the right thing," Lorne replied, hooking her arm through Sally's.

"Come on. We should be going now. Are you ready?" her mother asked.

"I suppose so. Thanks to you. Let's do this."

Lorne took a hanky from her pocket and wiped away the mascara that had smudged under Sally's eyes. "There you are. Beautiful as ever."

"Thank you, my dear friend. I miss you so much."

"Stop! Don't start us both crying again."

The three of them left the guest house and nipped across the road to the small chapel. Sally's eyes watered when she scanned the room and saw all her fabulous team and their families amongst the congregation. Beyond them, standing at the altar, were her father and Simon.

Half an hour later, the celebrant said the final part of the ceremony. "You may now kiss the bride."

"It's my pleasure," Simon said, a huge, proud grin on his face. "I love you, Mrs. Bracknall."

"I love you too, Mr. Bracknall, and always will."

THE END

NOTE TO THE READER

Dear Reader,

I hope you enjoyed this heart-wrenching tale? Is it time to stock up on the tissues?

Who knew such grave secrets could damage so many innocent lives.

As you can imagine this was one of the toughest books I've ever had to write.

But wait, Sally and her team are back in yet another heartbreaking tale, in Goodbye My Precious Child

Thank you as always for your support,

M A Comley

PS Reviews are like cupcakes to authors, won't you consider leaving one today?

Happy reading.

Made in the USA
Las Vegas, NV
17 February 2022